De...

...or picking up this Little B' ... one
of the great new titles f... our series of fun, page-turning
romance novels. Lucky you – you're about to have a fantastic
romantic read that we know you won't be able to put down!

Why don't you make your Little Black Dress experience
even better by logging on to

www.littleblackdressbooks.com

where you can:

* Enter our **monthly competitions** to win
  gorgeous prizes
* Get **hot-off-the-press** news about our latest titles
* Read **exclusive** preview chapters both from
  your **favourite** authors and from brilliant new
  writing talent
* Buy **up-and-coming** books online
* Sign up for an essential slice of romance via
  our **fortnightly email** newsletter

We love nothing more than to curl up and indulge in an
addictive romance, and so we're delighted to welcome you
into the Little Black Dress club!

With love from,

The *little black dress* team

Five interesting things about Nell Dixon:

1. I once crashed a Sinclair C5 into a tree. (Sinclair C5s were weird little concept cars that looked like a go cart.)

2. I'm scared of heights and got stuck on a rope bridge on an assault course and had to be rescued by a very nice army man.

3. I used to be a midwife and have delivered over a hundred babies.

4. I sing to the music in supermarkets, loudly and tunelessly. Strangely, my family prefer me to shop alone.

5. I have dyscalculia which means I can't remember numbers and often read them back to front.

Blue Remembered Heels

Nell Dixon

*little
black
dress*

First published in Great Britain in 2008 by
LITTLE BLACK DRESS
An imprint of HEADLINE PUBLISHING GROUP

A LITTLE BLACK DRESS paperback

1

ISBN 978 0 7553 4518 2

Typeset in Transit511BT by Avon DataSet Ltd,
Bidford-on-Avon, Warwickshire

Printed and bound in Great Britain by
Clays Ltd, St Ives plc

HEADLINE PUBLISHING GROUP
An Hachette Livre UK Company
338 Euston Road
London NW1 3BH

www.littleblackdressbooks.com
www.headline.co.uk
www.hachettelivre.co.uk

I'd like to dedicate this book to my good friend, Faith Muir, who listened patiently to my incoherent rambling about my story and nodded in all the right places. Her constant support, encouragement and belief in my abilities over the years has meant more to me than she'll ever know.

Acknowledgements

My grateful acknowledgements and thanks to the Romantic Novelists' Association for their help and support, especially the members of ROMNA for their collective in-depth knowledge of Wilmslow.

My thanks to the Romance Divas who helped me find out more than I will ever need to know about Catholic funeral rites in the absence of a body.

Thanks also to Allison Littlehales and Phillipa Ashley – a.k.a. the coffee crew for their support, coffee and lemon meringue pie sharing.

And big hugs and more thanks to my wonderful critique partner, Jessica Raymond, who is quite simply completely brilliant.

One minute I was standing on the high street, minding my own business, waiting for my bus. It was a nice day, no clouds or rain in sight, which makes what happened next all the more puzzling. *Wham!* Out of nowhere, I was struck down.

It sounds like a cliché but I don't remember much else, except the pain. Oh, and the man who gave me the kiss of life. I'd rather not remember him – he was a bit creepy. Then everything goes blurry until I wake up in the hospital with a strange name above my bed, my family sitting next to me and a scar on my neck.

'And what exactly do you think you're doing?'

Charlotte leaned back against the door of the powder room to stop anyone from disturbing us.

I opened my bag and pulled out my lipgloss. My older sister could be very scary when she was angry and right now she looked steaming mad.

'I didn't mean it. I just can't seem to stop myself.' The reflection in the oval gold mirror above the sink showed two high spots of colour on my cheeks. It also showed Charlie glowering at me in the background.

'I've spent weeks setting this job up, and I had to do most of the last part on my own because you were wallowing on the couch with Kip hanging on your every word.'

I finished touching up my lips as I waited for Charlie's temper to cool down. Only my sister could make me feel guilty about being found unconscious outside Debenhams after having been struck down by a bolt from the blue. The only reason I know I was hit by lightning is because there were witnesses, and the scar. Otherwise I might not have believed them.

'If you can't stick to the story then stay schtum. We are set to make a nice little sum out of this, but if your new-found conscience keeps twittering we won't make a penny and we'll end up in the clink instead.'

'It's not my fault. It's as if I haven't any control over what's coming out of my mouth.'

'Don't be ridiculous.'

'I'm not.' I wished I could explain it better to Charlie. It was hard not to feel resentful. She should know I never normally made careless mistakes or blabbed giveaway information when we were working.

Someone tried the door of the powder room. It bumped against the backs of Charlie's heels so she stepped forward to join me at the mirror. A buxom lady wearing a too-tight chiffon dress came in and shot us both a hard stare before disappearing into one of the cubicles.

'Just remember – keep it zipped,' Charlie hissed as I followed her back out into the lobby.

Our mark had waited for us in the bar area. It had been decorated according to some designer's vision of an old-fashioned gentlemen's club. All overstuffed seats and fake marble fireplace and crap lighting. I walked a couple of steps behind my sister and fumed silently.

'I do apologise. My assistant hasn't been well lately.' Charlie sank down gracefully on to one of the leather-padded armchairs and accepted a tall glass of gin and tonic from the man she'd come to scam.

The target flicked me a glance. I suspected he wouldn't have cared if I'd been dying of some rare tropical disease – it was Charlie he was interested in. Anyone who didn't know us would never guess we were sisters. Charlie is tall, dark and beautiful. That's why she's so good at what she does: enticing vain men to become hopelessly besotted with her so she can plunder their bank accounts. My skills, on the other hand, come from looking so ordinary. Average height, build, weight; blondish-brown hair – absolutely no qualities that would make me stand out in a crowd or a police line-up. I was the invisible woman.

For this particular job I had to play the part of Charlie's personal assistant. She had passed herself off as Lady Charlotte Bloom, which was a bit of a lark as although Charlie might be many things she was certainly no lady. Fortunately for us, the real Lady Charlotte was on safari in Africa and expected to remain there for another three weeks.

'Show Freddie the portfolio for the castle, Abigail.'

I fished about for the blue document folder that contained the details of Manydown Castle and tried to look like an efficient PA.

Freddie Davis was a self-made millionaire on the look out for a property to develop as his country home. There were lots of rumours about how he'd made his fortune and none of them were very flattering to his character. He was well known for being open to a dodgy deal so we were pretty sure he wouldn't worry about the ethics of the supposed sale. The idea of pulling a fast one over the tax man would be much more appealing.

He liked Charlie for her looks and alleged breeding, since he was anxious to move up the social scale. A hefty man in his late fifties with a round, florid face, he couldn't believe his luck at hooking up with someone like Charlie. It pandered to his ego, which was the size of a planet; it would serve him right when we took his money. He made the perfect mark.

Once Charlie had extracted a juicy 'deposit' for the castle we would be away and clear with the cash and Freddie would be history. I suppose it was a kind of rough justice – us doing to Freddie what he'd done to so many other people.

'My great-uncle Edward is anxious to keep this as a private sale, so I had a job to coax him into allowing me to show these to you. It would be simply too terrible if a treasured family home fell into the wrong hands.' Charlie sipped her drink and crossed her long, elegant legs.

'Oh, um . . . quite.' Freddie dragged his attention away from Charlie's legs and back to the folder containing the details for the castle. I prayed he wouldn't ask me any direct questions in case I did it again.

Told the truth, that is.

Not that I normally had any problem with lying. I'd made a career out of it, for heaven's sake. Even so, Charlie and I did have some morals – we never took money from anyone who couldn't afford it, and we never did anything that could cause physical harm to someone. As criminals go, we were very ethical.

We wouldn't be in this line of business at all if it weren't for Kip. He's our younger brother and he isn't . . . how do I put this . . . quite like other people. He has this dream of living on a farm, deep in the heart of the countryside, away from the city and all the hustle and bustle that so confuses and upsets him. Living in the city is making him ill. At the moment he never goes out, never meets anyone, and the longer we stay in London the worse he gets.

There have just been the three of us ever since Kip was a baby. Our mother had disappeared – vanished – when I was small. There was no hope of our helping Kip or escaping from the city via a 'normal' route. Office jobs simply don't pay the kind of money we need. We'd tried and failed in the past.

'I'd want to go and view the property,' Freddie said, looking straight at me with his avaricious little eyes.

'Of course. Great-uncle Edward is away at the moment but we'd be able to arrange for you to see the castle and land at the weekend, if you like.'

I breathed a small sigh of relief when Charlie answered before me. I hadn't said much to my sister about it yet, but I'd started to worry that being hit by that bolt a few weeks ago might have had some weird effect on me. Ever since, I haven't seemed able to stop telling the truth. In our business, this was likely to prove a major handicap. The argument in the cloakroom had been the first time I'd tried to broach the subject with Charlie.

I suppose you might think that getting zapped out of a clear blue sky on a crowded high street could be construed as an act of God. A kind of punishment for all the crimes I'd committed, even. I can tell you it was not at all nice to come round and find some ancient, smelly taxi driver giving me the kiss of life in front of a crowd of onlookers. My favourite gold earring had melted, I had a weird scar on my neck and my brain felt as if it had been boiled.

Charlie hadn't been impressed when my photograph had ended up splattered all over the papers. There had even been a small snippet on the evening news. The bag I'd had with me that day – and most of its contents – had been part of a fake identity from our last job. To the world at large, the lightning-strike victim had been Henrietta Jones, a twenty-two-year-old art restorer.

Just then I felt an odd prickling on my scalp. A sure sign of potential trouble. While Charlie continued to expound the virtues of dear Great-uncle Edward's castle, I glanced round the room to try to spot the cause of the warning. A tall man stood at the end of the bar with a bottle of lager in front of him. Good looking, but not head-turning. His eyes met mine and a chill ran down my spine.

The corners of his mouth lifted in a faint smile as he raised the bottle to his lips. He was fuzz, I could smell it, and handsome or not the fuzz always spelled trouble. Time to bail. Charlie and I had prearranged phrases to alert one another if we ever felt something was wrong.

I interrupted her spiel with, 'Excuse me, Lady Charlotte, but I believe your cousin Nigel may be calling on you today.'

She immediately acted on the cue by glancing at her tiny gold watch and making a little sound of dismay. 'Oh, how could I have forgotten? You will excuse me, won't you, Freddie? You know I'll make it up to you.' She gave him one of her trademark little-girl pouts and ran her hand seductively over his arm. 'I'll call you later with the details for the visit to Manydown.' She placed her empty glass on the table and rose to her feet.

Freddie immediately stood up and she leaned forward to kiss his cheek, leaving behind a tiny smudge of dark red lipstick. The man at the bar watched our little drama with a glint of amusement in his eyes, as if he knew exactly why we were leaving so suddenly. I had the uneasy feeling that he'd stored every detail of our meeting away in his mind for future use as evidence.

Charlie extracted the folder with the details of the castle from Freddie's fat little hands and passed it back to me. It didn't pay to leave loose ends, especially not ones that might have our fingerprints on them. Freddie saw us out to the front entrance, where the doorman called us a cab from the rank. Charlie managed to dodge an on-the-lips farewell smacker from Freddie and we slipped away on her promising of a dinner date later in the week.

The taxi driver dropped us a couple of streets away from the hotel, near a tube station from which we could get home. It was cheaper to go by train, and using more than one mode of transport made it less likely that anyone had followed us.

'Well? Why the alarm?' Charlie asked as soon as we were safely swallowed up in the crowd of anonymous commuters.

'Policeman at the bar.' I hung on tightly to one of the overhead straps.

My sister narrowed her dark green eyes. 'Mmm. Do you think it was set up?'

'I don't know, but he seemed very interested in our meeting.' My head ached from concentrating on being someone I wasn't and my fake glasses with their plain lenses had begun to annoy me.

'Better to be cautious. I'll sound Freddie out some more when he takes me out to dinner.'

Kip wasn't in the lounge when we got home, but his latest project stood uncovered on a table in the middle of the bay window.

'Kip, we're back!' It didn't look as if he'd done much work while we were out. His modelling knives and wood were still in a neat line next to his toolkit. When he didn't answer my call, Charlie went and knocked on the door of his room. Kip usually stayed in the lounge when we were out. He felt safe there, especially if he had something to work on. At the moment he had a balsa wood construction of the London Eye on the go.

'He's not in here.' I joined Charlie at Kip's door as she cautiously pushed it open a little wider. It took my eyes a moment to focus in the gloom. Kip always kept his curtains closed and the green glow from the tank where he kept his pet iguana bathed the room with a spooky alien light.

'Kip?'

A flicker of movement under the bed caught my eye. I lifted the Spiderman valance and hoped his pet rat, Claude, wasn't on the loose again. It was dark under there, but I could just make out the pale blue of my brother's favourite T-shirt.

'Kip, it's me, Abbey. We're home.' I stepped back as Kip wriggled forward and commando-rolled into the middle of the room, depositing his six-foot length at Charlie's feet.

She extended her hand to help him up. 'What happened?'

'Someone knocked on the door.' He pushed his glasses higher on to the bridge of his nose and blinked owlishly at Charlie.

Between us we steered him into the living room and plonked him down in a chair.

'How many times have we gone over this?' Charlie asked. Her voice was resigned. It did no good if you shouted at Kip. He would simply go and lock himself in the bathroom and refuse to come out. 'You don't have to answer the door. It's always locked. You can just stay nice and quiet in here.'

He nodded obediently at Charlie, just like always, but she and I knew he would have forgotten her instructions by the time the next caller came. It reinforced our determination to escape from the city and start a new life somewhere Kip would feel safe.

'How about I do fish fingers for supper?' If I made his favourite food it might help calm him down. Anything out of the ordinary, like a knock at the door when we were out, would unsettle him.

'And potato smiley faces?' he asked in a hopeful voice.

'Okay.'

I went into the kitchen to start supper while Charlie fired up the computer ready to trawl the Net in the name of research for our next project. Kip followed me in.

'Abbey, when will we be able to buy a farm?' He watched me place the fish fingers on the oven tray next to the smiley faces.

'Soon.' If our current project came off it would provide the deposit for Kip's dream home. Freddie could afford to buy a hundred farms, or castles for that matter. He really wouldn't miss the money Charlie planned to extract from him. The majority of Freddie's dosh had come from illicit land deals and letting properties at exorbitant rents to illegal immigrants; the rest had come from extortion and fraud. He wasn't a nice man and it would serve him right to get a taste of his own medicine.

Kip leaned against the countertop while I set the timer on the oven. His seventeen-year-old frame was far too skinny for his height and his skin looked pale from lack of sunlight.

'How's your model coming on?' I poured a couple of glasses of Coke and handed one to Kip.

'It's looking nice. I'm going to put lights on this one, Abbey.'

I'd guessed as much from the pile of library books on electric circuitry that he'd made me take out for him. Kip's hyper-intelligence when it came to things like electricity and computers had been part of the reason why he hadn't functioned well at school. That, and his lack of social awareness.

The educational psychologists had spent more time arguing about whether he should be in the gifted group or the autistic set than actually helping him. His red hair and the accompanying bullying hadn't helped much either, so all in all he hadn't spent much time in the classroom.

I wandered back into the lounge with my Coke and sat down on the sofa. My head ached from the hotel escapade so I closed my eyes and settled back for a minute.

I opened them again pretty quickly. It had happened again.

I swear to God that something had altered when that lightning bolt hit me. Everyone said I was lucky to be alive and the doctors had warned me that strikes often left odd side-effects behind. Now, every time I closed my eyes, I saw the same set of images. Just for a few seconds. Nothing scary, or that might hold any kind of significance. It wasn't even something I remembered happening. Perhaps that was why it had started to freak me out.

I saw the same vision every time. It was as if I was lying on the floor and I could see a pair of feet walking away from me. Women's feet, wearing navy blue high-heeled shoes.

I picked up my Coke from the coffee table and took a sip. Charlie gave a cackle of glee from her corner of the room.

'What have you found?' I knew that laugh; it meant she had a possibility in sight for the next job.

She reached her arms above her head in a satisfied stretch. 'Wait and see. We need to part Freddie from the contents of his wallet first.'

The oven timer pinged and I went back into the kitchen. Kip lay on the floor watching his tea cooking through the glass panel in the oven door.

'You don't need to do that.' I stepped over him and picked up the oven gloves.

He jumped up. 'I wanted to see how the light worked.'

I pulled the fish fingers and smiley faces out of the oven. 'Promise you won't mess with the cooker.'

Kip couldn't resist dismantling things to see how they worked. We'd lost a microwave and the toaster to his need to take things to pieces. Since we often needed an expert electrician in our job Charlie and I tried not to get mad at him, but it wasn't easy.

'*Kip.*' My voice held a note of warning.

'Okay, Abbey, I promise.'

I hoped he didn't have his fingers crossed behind his back. After installing Kip in front of the TV with his supper on a tray, I went to see what Charlie was up to. She frowned at the screen as I leaned over to see what she'd found.

'Well?'

'What's your knowledge of dogs like?' Charlie asked.

'I am not scooping poop!' I didn't like the speculative look in her eyes.

'But you like dogs?'

I scanned the screen for some clue to what she'd got in mind. It seemed to be a report about some middle-aged foreign woman and her charity work. 'Dogs are okay, I suppose.'

'Fab. You need to check out some more books from the library.'

Oh, goody, more research. 'What am I supposed to be this time?'

My brain still hurt from the art restoration job. Switching a painting and fencing the original to an Italian collector had netted us a tidy profit but had been riskier than normal. The more people that were involved in a scam the bigger the chance there was that something could go wrong.

'Get books on pet psychology and problem animals. I'll get what I can from the Net.'

'I'd like to point out that in addition to not

scooping poop I'm not prepared to get bitten.' I wasn't certain I liked the sound of this at all. My last close encounter with a dog had been with an Alsatian who had torn a chunk out of my jeans as I'd scrambled over a fence in an escape from good old PC Plod. That had been on one of our first jobs.

'Relax. It's just a means to an end, that's all. After we've finished with Freddie this should be a nice little break. Kip could do with a holiday.'

I glanced over to where Kip sat on the sofa munching contentedly on smiley faces while he watched some game show.

'Holiday where?' I suspected the kind of vacation my sister had in mind didn't involve buckets and spades and a sticky piece of Blackpool rock.

Charlie waved her hand airily. 'A spell out of town. Let the heat die down. I hear it's quite civilised now in the north.'

'I'd like to see the Angel of the North,' Kip announced.

'We'll try to fit it in,' she promised.

Charlie always behaved as if anything above Watford was as dangerous as the Amazon jungle. This had to be a pretty good job if she was prepared to risk leaving London.

'And what about you? What will you be doing while I'm faffing around with dogs?'

'Same thing I always do. I'll be entertaining the mark till we get our hands on the cash. Well . . . in

16

this case, gold.' Charlie's smile broadened. 'I always fancied becoming a WAG.'

Great. I get to scoop poop and she dates a footballer.

Pet psychology didn't seem likely to be the profession for me. I dropped the reference book and stretched my arms above my head. I'd never had a desire to become a female Doctor Dolittle.

'When will Charlie be back?' Kip asked as he soldered a piece of wiring, his tongue poking out and a frown on his brow as he concentrated. My big sister had trundled off to dinner with Freddie at some swanky restaurant wearing her favourite Chloé frock.

'Not sure. I'm packing this in for the night, though.' I'd had enough of reading about psychotic dogs and cats with low self-esteem.

Kip had finished the wooden structure of his model and had attached a small motor to the base to make it turn slowly like the real thing. 'I don't like Charlie being out late,' he announced.

I checked the time on the clock on the DVD player. 'It's only eleven.'

Kip ignored me and carried on fiddling with his electrical stuff. Charlie probably wouldn't be too much longer. Fortunately, Freddie liked a drink and she usually managed to get him sozzled enough for her to slip away without too much hassle. I still felt uneasy about the policeman I'd seen in the bar. The sooner this deal was sewn up the better. Even before my mishap with the lightning my conscience had been digging at me about my choice of career.

I hadn't planned on a life as a con woman any more than Charlie had. I'd wanted to work in an office and she'd wanted to be a beautician. But things don't always turn out the way you hope and when the extent of Kip's problems became clear to us we knew we had to think again. Our first scam happened by accident. Charlie's boss was ripping her off by pocketing her tips so we extracted some cash back to redress the balance.

It hadn't felt wrong at the time. We weren't hurting anyone – if anything, we felt quite Robin Hood-ish about it. We'd realised that this was a way we could strike a blow for all the little people who'd been cheated out of their precious wages. It also meant we could help Kip escape from the city, but lately I'd started to wonder if maybe we'd gone too far.

I wandered through to the kitchen and switched the kettle on. 'Do you want a cup of tea?'

'Yes, please, Abbey.'

The kitchen window had a view of the street. I watched a cab pull up down the road and Charlie climb out. She waited till the taxi had gone before she hurried towards our building, glancing up to wave at me before she slipped inside the front entrance and out of sight. I pulled another mug from the shelf and dropped a tea bag into it. A few minutes later I heard Charlie's key in the door of the flat.

'Whew.' She dropped her bag on the worktop and kicked her heels off into the corner of the kitchen.

'Sounds like you had a tough night.' I poured some boiling water on to the tea bags.

Charlie rolled her eyes as she passed me the milk. 'Honestly, that man should come with a health warning. He has more arms than an octopus and his chat-up lines are stuck somewhere in the seventies.'

'Did you manage to get the site visit set up?' I fished the tea bags out of the mugs and handed Charlie her drink.

'All set.' She grimaced as she wriggled her bare toes on the laminate floor.

'No trouble?'

'No. Why would there be?' She gave me a curious look.

'Look at my model, Charlie.' Kip beamed at her as she trailed into the lounge and flung herself down on the sofa. He flicked a switch and tiny blue lights appeared around the edge of his version of the London Eye as it rotated.

'That's beautiful, Kip.' Charlie and I spoke together.

The things Kip did just blew us away sometimes. He was so amazingly talented and yet so socially hopeless at the same time. He switched his model off and picked up his tea. 'Night.'

Charlie waited till he'd ambled off towards his bedroom. 'We need to hurry up and finish this job.' She picked at an imaginary piece of fluff on her dress.

'Why, what's up?' I kept my voice low so Kip wouldn't overhear us talking. The walls of our flat aren't very thick.

'I'm not sure.' She took a sip of her tea. It wasn't like Charlie to get rattled. I was the panicky one in our partnership.

'It's not too late to abort,' I suggested.

She shook her head. 'No, this is a good earner and we're almost there. Everything is set up. I checked and the real Lady Charlotte is still in Johannesburg. The site visit is planned for Sunday. You did go and suss out the place?' Her eyes narrowed.

'Yes. The housekeeper is away every Sunday from ten till six visiting her sister. I managed to get wax impressions of the keys and Kip has cracked the code for the alarm and CCTV.' I smiled. Hey, I was good at what I did, even if I said so myself.

'Great. Any problems?' She tucked her legs elegantly beneath her and peered at me over the rim of her mug.

My seat suddenly didn't feel quite so comfy. 'No, not really.' Maybe I should have said I *used* to be good at what I did. Since my lightning-strike episode everything had changed. The visit Kip and I had made to Manydown had been another example.

'What happened?' Charlie's voice took on a sharp edge.

'Nothing happened, not really.' Which was true. It was just another small incident, like the one when we'd been at the hotel the other day with Freddie.

'Abbey?' Charlie placed her mug carefully on the coffee table and focused all her attention on me.

'It wasn't anything, honestly.' I knew that look. It was the one she'd always used when we were growing up. The one that made you confess to all kinds of misdemeanours just to stop her from looking at you like that. And because I couldn't stop myself: 'It's just that ever since the accident I've been feeling a bit . . . odd.'

Charlie nodded. 'Go on.'

'I'm okay and work is fine. It's just . . .'

'For pity's sake, Abbey!'

'Well, sometimes when someone asks me something it's as if I have no control over what comes out of my mouth.'

Charlie blinked. 'What do you mean?'

'You remember when we met Freddie the other day?'

She pulled a face.

'And you got mad because he asked me where I lived?'

Charlie's brow creased. 'Yeah, what *was* that? You told him the area, and if I hadn't butted in you would have given him our whole address.'

'Well, that's just it. I couldn't stop myself. Normally I would have lied, gone with the cover story, but I really couldn't help it. I had to tell him the truth.'

'What are you saying?'

'When I went to the castle I'd been doing the stake-out for a while looking for my opportunity to get to the keys. I did my bewildered-and-lost-tourist bit and everything went fine. Then the housekeeper asked me a direct question and it happened again. I found myself being completely honest.'

The colour leached from Charlie's face. 'What did she ask you?'

'I was pretending to be French so I'd told her when I first met her that I was from Paris. But then she asked me when I had arrived in England.' I paused for a quick slurp of tea. I still hadn't figured out quite what had happened next.

Charlie glared at me.

'I couldn't help it. I opened my mouth intending to tell her that I was here for a few weeks on holiday, but instead I said I'd never been to France.'

'Oh my God!'

'Luckily, Kip's phone call came at just the right

time so it distracted her and she didn't hear what I said.'

Charlie groaned and ran a hand through her hair. 'This is crazy. It's happened, what? Twice now? And you say you can't not tell the truth when someone asks you a question?'

I nodded. 'It's been more than twice.'

'We should test this out. I mean, it could be one of those psychosomatic things. Maybe you should go see the doctor again.'

The rest of my tea had developed a scuddy surface. 'I don't know. The doctors said that sometimes people who've been struck by lightning have all kinds of odd stuff happen to them. It's a recognised side-effect of lightning strikes that they can cause these kinds of neurological idiosyncrasies. How would I explain it, anyway? "Hi, doc, I can't seem to tell lies any more"?'

'Okay.' She chewed her bottom lip and I could tell by the frown on her face that she was concerned. 'I need to think about this.'

I put my mug back in the kitchen. 'I'm off to bed.' I decided not to tell her about the dreams or she would have me whisked off to a psychiatrist.

Charlie blinked at me, the same way Kip does when he's distracted. 'Night.'

I didn't sleep too well. Ever since the accident the dreams have been getting worse. Well, not worse –

that's the wrong word. They're getting clearer and lasting a little longer each time but they are always the same. I'm lying down and I can see a shaft of light. I see legs, a woman's stocking-clad legs, walk into the light and pause. Whoever she is, she's wearing blue stiletto shoes with tiny gold buckles. Then she turns and walks away. The whole thing fades and goes black.

I don't see her face or even the hem of her skirt. Just the shoes, twinkling at me in the light. I'd decided against telling Charlie about the dreams. She was probably convinced I was a basket case anyway after our conversation last night. It sounded too odd to be true but the doctors had warned me before I was discharged that I might experience latent problems associated with the massive bolt of electricity that had charged through my brain. I suppose since the medical profession uses electric shock therapy for some kinds of problems it makes a kind of sense. Still freaky, though.

Kip was up and tucking into a bowl of cornflakes when I staggered into the kitchen.

'You look rough.'

'Thanks.' I grabbed a bowl from the cupboard and peered into the cereal packet.

'There's none left,' Kip announced through a mouthful of milk.

I put the bowl back and opened the biscuit barrel instead. 'I'll go shopping later.'

Kip carried on munching while I tried to find a

whole chocolate digestive out of the crumbs in the bottom of the barrel.

'I heard you and Charlie talking last night.'

That figures – Kip has ears like a bat. 'Kip, don't worry about it, okay? It's just some kind of temporary medical glitch, probably.'

Charlie and I were never quite sure how Kip would interpret the things he saw or heard. His intelligence and reasoning often meant he grasped concepts much more readily than we did but his emotions and his knack of taking everything literally could also send him into a flat spin.

'I know. I looked on Google this morning.' He set down his empty dish and wiped the milk from round his mouth with the back of his hand.

Kip probably knew more about this whole lightning thing than I did. He absorbed information like human blotting paper. No doubt he'd checked out every website he could find.

'It said you could experience all kinds of side-effects and they could affect any of your senses.'

I stopped rummaging in the biscuit barrel. 'You mean, like I could hear or see stuff that wasn't there?'

His eyes, so much like Charlie's in shape, seemed to burn into mine. 'Are you experiencing phenomena?'

'Yes,' I mumbled into the barrel. Damn it, there it was again. I'd wanted to say no!

Kip grabbed my hand and pulled me through into the lounge. 'This is amazing, Abbey.'

I'm glad someone thought all this weirdness was amazing.

'Tell me what you see. Or do you hear stuff? That would be cool if you heard stuff.' His eyes shone behind his glasses with the same fervent gleam he usually got when he acquired a new comic or started a fresh project.

'When I close my eyes I get this dream.' I told him about the woman.

'Wow.'

'Don't tell Charlie, will you? She'll only worry more about me if she knows.' Or have me at the nearest psychiatric hospital.

'I'll research it for you, Abbey. You can find out all kinds of things from dreams.' He looked so eager, I didn't have the heart to turn him down.

'Go ahead, if you want.' Maybe he'd find a way to stop me from dreaming, if it was a dream. Who knows, he might find something that would help with the other problem too. Perhaps a lie serum. My life had turned into a bad B movie. The only bright spot recently had been the cute guy at the hotel bar and he was a cop.

It took five trips to different charity shops before I managed to turn up the requisite wax jackets and green wellies for our trip to the castle. Charlie was adamant that we went for 'ye olde landed gentry' effect, as Freddie had to believe that the castle had been part of the same family's estate for generations. Which it had, of course, just not our family.

We were to meet Freddie down there, take him on a quick tour of the castle and grounds and then hustle him off for a long liquid lunch at a hotel just outside the town where Charlie was to lighten his wallet. When I'd visited the castle before in my guise as a French student I'd worn an auburn wig and coloured contact lenses so there shouldn't be much chance of anyone's recognising me. Charlie had emphasised to Freddie the need to keep the visit under wraps so as not to alarm the estate staff. Great-uncle Edward didn't want them upset.

Kip had cracked the alarm codes so all we had to do was wait for the housekeeper to trundle off then head down with our key, deactivate the alarm and greet Freddie when he turned up in his Jag. We'd installed Kip along the approach road to the estate in Charlie's minivan. He could keep watch, ensuring that no one disturbed us while Freddie did his tour of inspection.

'Do you think he'll be all right?'

Kip looked forlorn in our little white minivan with his binoculars slung round his neck as Charlie and I trudged off down the driveway towards the castle.

'He'll be fine. There aren't any people around

here. He likes the countryside and you said yourself he could use some fresh air.' Charlie stuck her hands in the pocket of her wax jacket and marched on.

I didn't think Kip would get all that much fresh air through the cracked-open window of the minivan. What he really needed was a holiday in the country or our long awaited and hoped for move to a smallholding in a nice rural location.

Charlie unlocked the castle door and I held my breath while she programmed in the code. Thankfully, the light on the alarm box turned green and no great clamour of bells or sirens went off above our heads. We'd memorised the floor plans ready for Freddie's arrival but I scooted off to do a quick recce before he turned up.

We didn't have to wait long before his silver Jag crunched its way over the gravel and stopped next to the front door.

'I'll do the talking,' Charlie hissed at me before she pasted her gracious hostess smile on her face and swept off to open the door.

I adjusted my Miss Marple-style tweed suit and pushed the plain-glass black-framed specs higher up the bridge of my nose. It was a bit irksome to keep being treated as if I was a liability but in fairness I was quite relieved that I wasn't being asked to do more than trail around after them and offer refreshments at appropriate intervals.

'Freddie, darling, come in.'

Freddie loosened the buttons on his cashmere overcoat and looked up appreciatively at the portraits lining the walls of the hallway. 'Very nice.' He nodded his head in approval as Charlie beamed at him.

'Would you like a cup of tea or coffee before I take you off on the grand tour?'

I tried to look as if I frequently made drinks for guests at the castle and attempted to remember where I'd seen tea bags in the huge kitchen.

Freddie rubbed his hands together, making the chunky gold bracelet jangle on his wrist. 'No, we'll just crack on, shall we? I know how keen you are to keep this visit under wraps.'

'I told Great-uncle Edward you could be trusted to be discreet. If word of this sale got out before everything was signed and sealed it would just be too terrible. The staff would be upset and everyone would think poor old Uncs was on his uppers.'

Freddie gave a self-conscious laugh as Charlie slipped her arm through his and led him into the receiving room. I followed behind them for the next couple of hours while Charlie gave him the full sales patter. I sent Kip a quick text while Freddie and Charlie were up on the roof admiring the view of the estate.

Are you okay?

Lots of lovely birds. I'm feeding them my sandwich.

I relaxed a little once I knew he was all right. So long as he didn't get so distracted by the wildlife that he forgot he was supposed to be our lookout.

Freddie seemed more interested in admiring Charlie's bum than the solid oak balustrades as he followed her down the stairs. We ended up in the library and I poured Freddie a glass of whisky from the rather naff globe-of-the-world storage cabinet I'd found in there.

'Well, everything seems to be in good order,' Freddie announced as he rocked back and forth on the soles of his feet in front of the Portland stone fireplace. He clearly had himself in the role of castle overlord already.

'I knew you and Manydown would be a match made in heaven.' Charlie leaned forward to pick up her glass from the coffee table and I noticed she'd undone an extra button on her shirt.

'I had my surveyor look over those reports you sent me, Charlotte. He was very impressed.' Freddie took another slurp of whisky and gazed round the room with a proprietorial air.

'You must come and have a look at the lake before we head off. You said you liked to fish, I think?' Charlie drained her glass and handed it to me. Freddie followed suit without as much as a thank you.

'Abigail, I'll leave you to lock up. Oh, and remind me to instruct Mrs Burton to have the curtains in the great hall cleaned.'

'Yes, Lady Charlotte.'

'I've booked lunch at the Baliton Arms. Such a darling place.' Charlie slipped her arm through Freddie's.

'Will your assistant be joining us?' Freddie flicked me a dismissive glance. I prayed he wouldn't ask me how I was getting back to town.

'No, she has too much to do here before she rejoins me this evening.'

The mobile, set to vibrate, rumbled gently against my hip. Kip's signal to alert us.

'My lady, I believe the ground near the lake is quite boggy at the moment. Perhaps Mr Davis would see the estate better if he took the drive by the woods.' We had to get Freddie's car moved from the front of the castle and the place locked back up before anyone came down the drive. Luckily, Kip had a delaying tactic to postpone any such occurrence.

'Oh, what a nuisance. Still, we'll have more time for lunch if we take the car.' Charlie winked at me as she led Freddie out of the front door. I locked it behind them then stuffed the dirty glasses back inside the globe, hoping poor Mrs Burton wouldn't get into trouble when they were discovered.

I'd just managed to reset the alarm and hide in the shrubbery when Mrs Burton's little red Fiat Panda pulled up in the spot where Freddie's Jag had been parked only moments before. The housekeeper emerged carrying a large bag and unlocked the door.

As soon as she'd gone inside I scuttled out of my hiding place and legged it down the drive under the cover of the trees. I hadn't realised it was possible to move so quickly in a tweed skirt.

Kip slid open the side door of the minivan when I banged on the panel.

'That was too close for comfort.' I wheezed the words out, breathless from sprinting through the undergrowth to reach him. Kip, always prepared, passed me my inhaler and I took two puffs.

'You should take this with you.' He waited for me to regain my ability to breathe.

'The housekeeper nearly caught us. Freddie and Charlie had only just pulled away when she rolled up.' The tightness in my chest eased and I slumped back in my seat.

'I used the binoculars and called as soon as I saw her car on the top road. Plus, she had to stop to clear the branches I'd left on the track to slow her down.'

'Stupid woman wasn't meant to be back yet anyway. Every other Sunday she's been gone all day.' I plucked some leaves out of my hair and wriggled into position on the driver's seat. The pressure in my chest relaxed and I dropped the inhaler into my bag.

Kip shrugged and took another swig from one of the cans of pop we'd left with him. 'It's nice here in the countryside. I was pretending we had our farm.'

I looked through the windscreen. Ahead of us the road to the castle curved upwards through the trees like a silver ribbon on a green blanket. In the distance I could see the lake sparkling in the sunshine. Birds twittered in the branches next to the van and a small grey squirrel darted up the trunk of a nearby oak. If Charlie managed to get some money out of Freddie over lunch our farm would be a step nearer to reality. The security of a permanent home that we all longed for . . .

'I don't suppose there are any sandwiches left? I'm starving.' My stomach gave a growl as I looked at the bits of tinfoil that lay crumpled and discarded on the floor of the van.

'Sorry, Abbey.'

'Pick this mess up.'

He bent and gathered together the foil.

'We need to set off for home. I'll call at the bakery in the village for something. We should be okay as there's no CCTV round here.' Charlie wouldn't be pleased if she knew we planned to go into Manydown, but there would be surveillance at the motorway service stations and I was absolutely starving.

'We're supposed to go straight home,' Kip warned me as we approached the edge of the village.

'And you were supposed to keep me a sandwich!'

Manydown was a typical country village. It boasted a pub, a church, a bakery, a general store, a butcher, a greengrocer, an ironmonger and a couple of clothes shops. I parked the minivan in the small car park behind the church and trotted across the street to the bakery.

Of course it was shut. I'd forgotten about it being Sunday. The small general store at the end of the road looked as if it was open so I headed down the street in the hope that they would at least have some crisps and chocolate.

At first glance it looked pretty deserted when I stepped through the old-fashioned door complete with jingly bell. A middle-aged woman at the counter was serving an elderly man with whisky and cigarettes while the rest of the shop appeared to be empty. I picked up one of the battered wire baskets from the end of the counter and looked along the shelves for something to keep my stomach quiet on the journey home.

The tinkle of the shop bell signalled the arrival of another customer just before I spotted some tubes of Pringles right up on the top shelf.

'Allow me.' A masculine arm reached over my head and handed me a tube of cheese flavour.

'Thank you . . .' The words died on my lips as I turned to look at my snack saviour. Holy crap, it was the same man who'd been in the hotel bar when

Charlie and I had been setting up the sting on Freddie!

'You look familiar. Have we met?' Dark brown eyes the colour of melted chocolate gazed into mine. A shiver ran down my spine and I knew he was being sarcastic. He knew damn well where he'd seen me before.

'I saw you in a hotel bar once.' Crapity crap crap – why couldn't I regain control over my mouth? Charlie would kill me and we were all going to go to jail if I didn't learn to zip it. He smelled delicious though: masculine and woody. I knew I was in trouble and not just because I couldn't keep my mouth shut.

His eyes narrowed and I guessed my openness had caught him off guard. 'Yes, you were with a very pretty dark-haired girl.'

'My sister Charlie.' I smiled at him even as I cursed myself for being unable to stop blabbering like an idiot. Typical – even the coppers fell for my sister. That idea dampened my spirits somewhat.

'And a Mr Freddie Davis was with you?'

'Yes.' Blast.

'Are you and your sister friends of Mr Davis?' His tone was casual but I knew a cop interrogation when I heard it. The problem was I couldn't re-engage my mouth with my brain.

'Business only.'

He might have a very sexy voice for a cop, but all

the same I had to get out before he could ask me anything else. I'd said far too much as it was.

'Nice meeting you but I'll have to go; my brother's waiting for me.' I squeezed past him. The heat from his body shimmered into mine in the confined space of the aisle and I bolted through the tinned goods section to the till. Thank God I had cash. I plunked my Pringles in front of the cashier and added a couple of Crunchie bars from the display on the counter.

With the change in my pocket I made for the door, only to find Mr Sexy Voice waiting for me.

'Don't I even get to know your name?' He pulled the door open.

'Abbey Gifford.' I stepped outside, praying he wouldn't try to follow me.

'Mike Flynn. Perhaps we'll meet again?' Cute little crinkles formed at the corners of his eyes as he smiled.

'Maybe.' I was flirting with the enemy. That bolt of lightning had a lot to answer for.

I scuttled off in the opposite direction from the van in case he was still watching me. As soon as it seemed safe I doubled back down a side street and rejoined Kip.

'You were ages.'

'The bakery was closed.' I popped the top off the Pringles and stuffed a handful of the crisps into my mouth.

Kip pinched one and nibbled on it, a thoughtful expression on his face. 'What else happened, Abbey?'

Now the crisps had restored my blood sugar I felt calmer. 'I saw someone I knew.'

Kip's eyes widened behind his glasses. 'That's bad, isn't it?'

'Maybe.' I opened the glove compartment. I kept a small stash of accessories for emergency use in there. Once my hair was hidden under a spotted headscarf, huge dark sunglasses covered half of my face and garish orange lipstick was plastered on my lips, we were ready to roll.

'Who did you see?'

'A policeman.' I didn't want to tell him that but he'd asked me the question knowing I'd be unable to lie to him.

'You and Charlie won't get sent to prison, will you?'

'Not if we can help it.'

Kip stuffed his distinctive auburn curls under a baseball cap and slouched down in the passenger seat. I drove out of the village keeping a sharp eye out for Mike but didn't see any sign of him. Unanswered questions raced around my head as I drove. Why was Mike following us? Or was he following Freddie? I knew Freddie had his fat little fingers in all sorts of pies and most of them were not exactly above board. My palms felt sweaty against the plastic of the steering wheel. The sooner we finished this job the better.

We'd barely made it out of the village and on to the dual carriageway when the mobile went off. Kip answered, as I was busy concentrating on the road. 'Hello . . . Okay, I'll tell Abbey.' He turned the phone off.

'What is it?' A lorry cut me up.

'Charlie wants us to collect her on our way home. She's having trouble with Freddie.'

I flipped the lorry driver a V-sign and roared off down a side road. 'Good job she rang before we hit the motorway.' I wasn't too worried about Charlie. She was more than capable of handling Freddie but it wouldn't be good to antagonise him before he'd handed over the cash. Still, my recent encounter with Mike had me rattled. 'Is she still at the hotel?'

'Yes.' Kip started giving me directions.

From what I could remember of the Baliton when we'd cased it out there was only one small car park to the side of the dining room. We wouldn't be able to pick Charlie up from there in the van. We couldn't risk Freddie's associating her with a vehicle, or seeing me. I'd have to call Charlie when we got nearer to the hotel and work out what we were going to do to extricate her.

'It should be down the next street, on the right.' Kip closed the map book.

I slowed to a crawl. The Baliton was in a sleepy little market town not much larger than Manydown. It might appear pretty quiet but I was prepared to bet there were any number of nosy parkers peering out from behind the lace-curtained cottage windows facing the high street. I stopped outside Betty's Knit and Baby Shop and called Charlie on her mobile.

She answered straight away. 'Where are you?'

'We're in the high street. What do you want us to do?'

'I'm in the lobby; Freddie's in the bar. I've got the money in my handbag. He's busy celebrating.'

I could hear the buzz of people in the background. 'I can't bring the van up, it's too noticeable. You'll have to come to us. Go back in to Freddie – I'll move the van to a side street and come up to signal you.'

'Hurry.' She clicked off, but not before I'd heard Freddie's slurred tones calling her to have a drink.

Kip fidgeted in his seat as I wriggled out of my tweed skirt and into a pair of jeans. With my jacket discarded and still wearing the headscarf and sunglasses I looked a completely different person from the prim and proper secretary of that morning's adventures.

I'd pulled the van into a side road near the Baliton. It had the advantage of being near some open ground so there was a reduced risk of some unseen person's taking an unhealthy interest in what we were doing. Even so, I hoped it wouldn't take long to get Charlie. It sounded as though she had the money we needed to clear up and get out.

'You won't be long, will you, Abbey?' Kip's face wore a worried expression and he wrung his hands together as I touched up my orange lipstick.

'We'll be back before you know it.' I gave his leg a pat and slipped out of the van, locking the door behind me.

The Baliton was a large mock-Tudor building with ideas of grandeur. It was a popular eating and drinking place with both locals and people from the surrounding area. The bar was full. Evidently, Sunday lunchtime was prime drinking time at the hotel. I sidled into the room and looked round for Charlie.

It took a moment for my eyes to adjust to the gloom of the subdued lighting and the sheer volume of people jostling about the bar. All the seats appeared to be occupied and the piped music was barely audible above the chatter. Freddie was seated on a large winged armchair near the window and seemed to have acquired a group of drinking buddies – all middle-aged and florid-faced. Very similar to Freddie, really.

Charlie stood beside him, nursing what looked like a gin and tonic. Every now and then she appeared to force a smile as the group roared with laughter. It sounded as if Freddie was in full flow with his 'wonderful me' stories. There was nothing Freddie's ego liked more than an attentive audience all telling him how marvellous he was. It was one of the attributes that had made him ideal as a mark – that and his greed.

I started to work my way round the room, so I could give her the cue to escape. Three-quarters of the way round I froze. A figure that had started to become all too familiar was leaning against the bar. Mike, the copper. Hell. Now what was I supposed to do? I saw Charlie check her watch and stifle a yawn. She hadn't noticed me amongst the crowd. It didn't look as if she'd clocked Plod of the Yard, either.

How had Mike managed to get to the Baliton so quickly? And how had he known to come here? The sooner I could get Charlie and the money out of the bar the better, or we would be caught red-handed with the loot. A shiver ran down my spine. No way was I prepared to do time for ripping off a bloke who'd ripped off hundreds more people than Charlie and I ever could.

I managed to position myself behind a rotund gent in a hacking jacket and watched Mike to see what he was doing. To the casual observer he seemed to simply be sipping his bottled lager and helping himself to peanuts from the dishes on the bar. Every few minutes, however, he looked across towards Charlie and Freddie with a speculative look on his face.

Normally I would have had every confidence in my ability to get past him unrecognised. He shifted his gaze in my direction and I ducked behind my human shield. The man must have radar. I swear he knew I was there. Every cell in my body felt as if he was watching me.

A skinny woman with dyed blond hair dug me in the ribs as she squeezed past to get to the bar. My shield moved, leaving me temporarily exposed. Mike looked directly at me and I was glad of my sunglasses. For a moment I thought he'd recognised me and I held my breath. He seemed to stare at me for a fraction of a second longer than was really necessary but then he returned his attention to my sister.

I worked my way behind a crowd of rowdy lads who looked as if they were a Sunday football team, and risked another peep. Charlie looked a little desperate. Freddie shouted for another round of drinks and the noise from his entourage went up a notch when the glasses arrived.

I worked my way back out of the room and into the lobby. It was too risky to call Charlie's mobile and not safe to linger where the receptionist might get nosy, so I stepped outside to think. A gravel path led from the front entrance round the side of the hotel.

After a quick look round to make sure no one was watching me, I set off along it.

Charlie was still standing in the same position next to the window, shifting her weight from foot to foot. I tapped gently on the glass near her shoulder and darted back a little way in case I'd attracted anyone else's attention by mistake.

It didn't look as if anyone was about to look through the window. They were all too intent on enjoying Freddie's hospitality. I could hear the noise and guffawing from my spot amidst the bedding plants. It sounded as if Freddie was telling his dreadful sexist and racist jokes again.

I knocked again, a little louder. Charlie looked over her shoulder, her eyes widening when she twigged it was me. Freddie turned his head to speak to her and I ducked back, plastering myself against the brickwork before he noticed me.

I waited for my heart rate to slow down and then risked another peep. Charlie glanced round, I nodded my head towards the front entrance and she winked. She emerged from the front door just a few seconds later. I waited to make certain she was alone before calling to her from my hiding place by the laurel bushes.

'Come on, let's go. Freddie thinks I've gone to the ladies.' Charlie hurried towards me as fast as her heels would allow.

'No one's following you, are they?'

She looked over her shoulder. 'No. Why would they?'

'I'll tell you when we're out of here. You go first.'

Charlie took off down the drive just as Mike appeared at the front door of the hotel. He strode down the steps in the direction of the car park. Once he was safely out of the way I pulled my headscarf further forward and raced after my sister.

'I'll drive.' Charlie whisked the keys to the van from my hand as I collapsed wheezing next to Kip.

'Get going,' I panted. Kip helped me fasten my seatbelt. My hands were shaking too much to manage it on my own.

'What's wrong?' Charlie forced the van into first gear, grinding the box as she did so.

'Policeman, Mike, at the bar.'

'Next left,' Kip called out. The tyres of the van screeched and I was thrown against him as Charlie swung the van round the corner.

'Police? How do you know his name?' she demanded as we lurched over a pothole.

'Slow down! I ran into him in Manydown.' I told her what had happened in the general store.

Charlie's lips compressed into a thin line. I knew that look – it didn't bode well.

'What were you doing in Manydown? No, don't bother, I'd rather not know. So, you told him our names and that we were seeing Freddie on business? For God's sake, Abbey.'

'Motorway coming up,' Kip interrupted.

'I couldn't help it.' I did my best to defend myself.

'Well, that makes me feel a whole lot better,' Charlie snapped. She cranked the van up to seventy to pass a caravan.

'It's a well-recognised phenomenon. I researched it on the Internet,' Kip chipped in as we diced with death in the fast lane.

'What, that being hit by lightning makes you blab all your secrets and chat up policemen?' My sister can be very sarcastic.

'That's not fair, Charlie. I really can't help it.'

'I've found some ideas for therapy that we can try.' Kip loved trying things out that he'd found on Google or Wikipedia. The problem tended to be that if something was on the Net or on TV, Kip believed it as gospel. He was an advertiser's dream consumer and we'd had to ban him from accessing the shopping channels to avoid the threat of bankruptcy.

'Maybe you should see a doctor or a therapist.' Charlie hit the brakes as the traffic in front suddenly slowed.

'How can I do that? I'd tell the truth in reply to any question about my medical history and then what would happen?'

'Abbey's right.' Kip blinked at me, his eyes alight with enthusiasm. 'We can do the treatments at home. Honestly, I found lots of things that might help.'

'Well, we need to do something. You're a bloody liability at the moment.' Charlie glared at me.

The rest of the journey home was spent in an uncomfortable silence. As soon as we got indoors, Charlie took herself off for a bath. I dropped my bag on the sofa and went to put the kettle on.

'I really think I can help you, Abbey.' Kip followed me into the kitchen. 'I've been looking up dream sites as well, and all the research indicates that the blue-shoe thing could be a repressed memory.' He waved his hands in excitement.

'Keep your voice down! I don't want Charlie to know about the shoe business. She doesn't really believe that I can't help telling the truth when I answer questions so she'll definitely think I've lost it if she knows about the visions as well.' I spooned sugar into Kip's mug.

'It may even be a past-life memory.' He trailed after me as I went back into the lounge with my tea.

I plopped myself down on the sofa and swung my legs up on to the armrest. 'It might be an old advert from the TV that I saw as a kid – or a film or something. That's much more likely than a past life.' Reincarnation had never been something that featured highly on my radar.

Kip sat cross-legged on the floor like a skinny and earnest Buddha. 'But we should still try regression and see if it works.'

'I don't know.' It all sounded crazy to me, but then

again, before I got frazzled by a meteorological catastrophe I would have scoffed at the idea that I'd be desperate enough to seriously consider Kip's suggestion.

'You haven't anything to lose, Abbey.' Kip sipped his tea and the steam fogged up his lenses.

'I don't have to be hypnotised or anything, do I?' I didn't fancy the idea of being put into a trance. Especially when the person doing the hypnotising was a seventeen-year-old geek with a limited attention span.

'It says you go into a relaxed state of mind. Unless you'd like me to properly hypnotise you into a deep trance? I've practised on Claude.' He looked hopefully at me.

I swallowed some more of my tea. 'Claude is a rat. I don't think they have the same neurological responses as humans.'

Muffled thumps and curses came from the direction of the bathroom.

'Speaking of rats, it sounds as if he's made a nest in the bathroom again. You'd better go and put the kettle back on.'

Kip slouched back to the kitchen just as Charlie burst into the lounge, wrapped in her Betty Boop dressing gown with a pink towel round her head.

'Claude?'

She huffed down on the armchair and began rubbing at her hair. 'Kip and his blasted animals . . .'

'Did Freddie pay the full ask for the deposit?' Normally at this point Charlie would have been gloating about our success and getting her notes out for the next job.

She stopped towelling her hair. 'Thirty grand in cash. It's in my handbag in a brown envelope. Pity we can't risk pushing for a full sale and taking him for the million.'

Kip handed her a mug of tea by way of a peace offering. I just looked at her. There was no way I was prepared to go along with a scam that size.

'I'm not happy about this policeman – this Mike, whoever he is.' Charlie put her drink down on the coffee table and pulled her detangling comb from her dressing-gown pocket.

'Well, there's not a lot we can do about him.' I didn't like the speculative glint in her eye. It was a shame Mike was the enemy; he was kind of cute.

'Mmm.' She didn't sound convinced.

Kip and I exchanged glances. We knew that look. It meant trouble.

Charlie took the money to the bank bright and early the next day. We have a business account where we pay in our profits. Then Charlie draws out our expenses and wages and things. Kip has a spreadsheet with everything coded. He's very good at that kind of stuff. We even have an accountant who audits our figures. On the surface we run a very profitable public relations and marketing business doing freelance jobs for high-class customers.

I knew Charlie was busy planning our next job, the dog-whispering project. It still bothered me. Kip is great with animals, but apart from occasionally feeding Claude and the rest of his menagerie I've never had much to do with them. Well, apart from the police dog, but that wasn't a good memory. I'd been feeling increasingly uneasy about our con jobs too. Maybe my long-neglected conscience was finally beginning to stir. I couldn't help but wonder if my inability to lie was some kind of subconscious rebellion.

'I've got you some info on the regression therapy.' Kip brandished a bundle of papers at me.

I'd hoped he would go off the idea. I should have known better. 'I'm not sure about this, Kip. It says it's hypnosis here.'

'It also says you can't be made to do or say anything you don't want to. You do want to get better, don't you?' He poked at the paper with his finger to underline his point about the safety of the procedure. 'And . . . ta-da!' He reached behind his back and waved a CD at me like a magician producing a bunch of flowers from a hat.

'What's that?' I hoped it wasn't some of that whale music. If he put anything like that on I'd go off into a fit of giggles instead of a state of relaxation and then he'd get the hump.

'It's a special CD. It explains everything and gets you in the right frame of mind. Go on, Abbey, give it a go.'

The cover of the case looked to be all kosher and above board.

'We might even find out some more about your shoe dream.' Kip couldn't keep the eagerness out of his voice.

I did want to know more about the dream or vision or whatever it was. I'd been trying to convince myself it was some film I'd seen once, maybe a Hitchcock one, that had started some mad play-loop in my brain. And yet the thought that it was somehow significant, that it meant something important, kept nibbling away at me. As if it was an event I needed to remember.

'You're sure it's not dangerous?' I took the disc from his hand.

'Cross my heart and hope to die.' His eyes sparkled.

'Okay, tell me what I have to do.'

We trooped into my bedroom and I drew the curtains. The instructions that had come with the disc suggested subdued lighting. I switched on the mood light Kip had given me for Christmas. Blue and pink circles of light floated up the walls and across the ceiling.

'I feel stupid already.' I lay on the bed and Kip popped the CD into my player before positioning himself by my feet clutching a spiral notepad and a biro.

'You are going to take this seriously, aren't you?' he warned me.

'Yes.'

He pressed the play button and we waited for the instructions to begin. The music started and I stifled a giggle. It wasn't whales, but some of that weird Celtic stuff – all mournful and creepy. Kip glared at me in the gloom and I swallowed my laughter to concentrate on the speaker.

I must have been tired because my eyelids started to droop while I listened to the monotone drawl of the man on the disc.

'You will stop being truthful.' Kip's voice sounded distant, strange, like the man on the machine.

'I'll stop being truthful,' I repeated dutifully. Somewhere in the distance I heard the front door bang. I focused on the voice and the positive affirmations.

My eyes closed and I was back. But back where?

'Tell me where you are, Abbey.'

'On the floor.'

It was true. I wasn't lying on my nice, soft mattress any more. Instead, the sensation of lying on hard, carpet-covered floorboards filled my senses. I could feel heat on my face as if I were next to a gas fire.

'What can you see?'

I knew what was coming. 'I can see a doorway into a hall.' I couldn't hear the Celtic music any more. There was the sound of a television and now the woman's feet were coming towards me.

'Describe what you feel.'

'I want . . .' I wanted the woman to pick me up. Tears were rolling down my face. The feet grew nearer. High-heeled dark blue stiletto shoes with little gold buckles. They were so pretty. The buckles glittered in the firelight. A strong smell of perfume filled the air.

'Abbey, what can you see?'

She was going. Disappointment filled me. I wanted her to stay.

'Abbey?'

The feet walked away from me into the hall and I wanted to run after her. Then she was gone.

'Abbey?' Kip's voice sounded urgent.

The CD had stopped. I opened my eyes and found my cheeks were wet with tears.

'Oh, Kip. I think it was Mum.'

Suddenly Charlie was in the doorway, still wearing her coat, her face pale in the half-light. 'What the hell are you two doing? What's this about Mum?'

Kip scrambled to his feet. 'We were trying regression therapy.'

Charlie snapped on the overhead light. I pulled some tissues from the box next to the mood lamp and dried my eyes.

'Why is Abbey crying?' Her hands balled into fists as she placed them on her hips while she waited for us to speak.

'It's not Kip's fault.' It felt as if we were little kids again and I was protecting Kip from Charlie's wrath after he'd broken yet another household appliance.

She stalked over to the window and threw open the curtains. 'I knew this half-baked hokey stuff from the Net would cause trouble.'

'It's not half-baked. It's proper science.' Kip's voice squeaked up in pitch and his Adam's apple bobbed up and down.

'He's right. I didn't tell you before, but it's not just the truth thing that's the problem. I've been having these flashbacks.'

Charlie turned to face me. 'What do you mean, flashbacks?'

'Ever since I got hit by the lightning I've been seeing this scene in my head, whenever I close my eyes or start to relax. It's always the same.' I told her about the shoes.

As soon as I'd finished she sank down on to the end of the bed and put her head in her hands. 'Oh my God.'

Kip fidgeted by the doorway, his movements betraying his anxiety.

'Charlie? Are you okay?' I sat up and tried to peer at her face. I'd never seen her like this, not even when we'd realised Mum wasn't coming back, or when we'd been in care or at Aunty Beatrice's or anything.

Charlie had been really tough when the police had arrived after a neighbour had realised we were alone and alerted the authorities. She'd fought to keep us together at the children's home while the social workers and police had looked for a relative who might take us all in. I'd been very young then; I remember people clucking around me and calling me a 'poor little love'. Then Aunty Beatrice had come forward and we hadn't been allowed to talk about Mum or what had happened. Now everything was coming back, all those horrible, painful memories.

Kip's foot beat an involuntary tattoo on the carpet as he struggled with his distress.

'It's all right, Kip.' I tried to reassure him and to keep the alarm out of my voice.

'Mum had blue shoes like that. They were her best shoes, the ones she wore when she was going on a date. The night she left she was wearing them.' Charlie's voice wobbled and she paused for a second before she went on. 'I used to dress up in them and wear her bead necklaces when she wasn't looking.' She lifted her head and I saw that her eyes were full of tears.

'I'm sorry, Charlie. I didn't mean it.' Kip bolted from the room and I heard the sound of the bathroom door being locked. I passed Charlie the tissues and she had a good sniffle before blowing her nose.

'He's locked himself in the bathroom,' she said.

'Bugger. I could really use a wee as well.'

She grinned at me and gave me a hug. 'I'm sorry. It takes me by surprise sometimes. I don't think about Mum or wonder what happened to her very much any more, but then something will trigger off the memories and make me think. Oh, Abbey, what *did* happen to her?'

It had been a long time since Charlie and I had last discussed Mum. 'I don't know. I don't even know if what I'm remembering now is significant. I always thought she'd never have left us willingly.'

Charlie sighed. 'That's what I always thought too, but after living with Aunty Beatrice . . .' She rolled her eyes and we both shuddered.

'She never had a good word to say about Mum,' I said. That was an understatement. Aunty Beatrice never had a good word to say about anyone.

Aunty Beatrice had meant well. She'd told everyone who'd listen that she'd done her Christian duty by us. In fairness to her she'd clothed us, fed us and given us a home where at least we could all be together. There just hadn't been much affection or fun. She'd also never really understood about Kip, wanting to dose him with the medication the doctor had prescribed until he was like a zombie. We'd had to get out and take Kip with us before it was too late.

'Even so, perhaps we ought to go and pay her a visit. We're long overdue for asking some questions.'

I wasn't filled with joy by Charlie's suggestion. It was hard to believe that Aunty Beatrice and Mum could have been related at all, let alone been sisters.

Been sisters?

When had I accepted that Mum was dead? All through my teens I'd clung to the belief that she would come back. That one day she'd walk through the door and into our lives and everything would be okay again. It had kept me going through some of the bleakest moments in my life. She couldn't be dead.

'Let's go and talk Kip out of the bathroom.' Charlie's voice broke into my thoughts.

'And let's not mention visiting Aunty Beatrice.' She wasn't Kip's most favourite person: he was always scared she might make him live with her again.

It took half an hour and the promise of alphabetti spaghetti for tea to persuade Kip to relinquish the bathroom. Charlie grabbed a sandwich and settled in front of the computer to work out the finer points of the next job. Kip disappeared to his bedroom to share a packet of Wagon Wheels with Claude and I settled down for more research on pet psychology.

After reading a chapter devoted to appetite disorders in German shepherds I started to feel peckish myself. I wasn't craving the book's suggestions of minced chicken or T-bone steaks, but I did have a hankering for scrambled egg on toast. The toaster was still out of action from when Kip had decided to investigate the heating element, however, so I slung some bread under the grill instead.

I was getting the eggs from the fridge when I happened to glance out of the kitchen window. At first I thought I was mistaken but another look confirmed what I thought I'd seen. Mike, the cop, was out there, examining the tax disc on Charlie's minivan.

5

I peered out round the edge of the kitchen blind.
Mike appeared to be making notes in a little book
as he prowled around the minivan. My heartbeat
speeded up to the point where I thought I would be
physically sick. It looked as if Charlie and I were
goners.

'Abbey, what the hell are you doing? The toast's on
fire!' Charlie grabbed the grill pan complete with
flaming toast and dropped it into the sink. Before I
could stop her she threw open the kitchen window to
release the smoke. The smoke alarm started to cheep
and it took me a minute to find the reset button to
silence the noise.

Mike raised his head at the sound of the window
opening and looked straight into my eyes.

'Crap.' I ducked back into the room, coughing
my lungs up with the acrid smell of cremated
bread.

'What were you mooning over out there?' Charlie
went to look for herself. 'You could have burned the
place down.'

'It's Mike, the policeman I told you about.' I put my hand on her arm to stop her.

'What the hell is he doing poking about round here? You didn't tell him where we lived, did you? Bloody hell, Abbey!'

'Of course I didn't. He was looking at the minivan. Maybe our number plate's been recognised.'

There was a loud knock on the front door.

Charlie glared at me. 'Stay out of sight and leave this to me.'

I slipped off to my bedroom, making sure that the door was slightly ajar so I could hear the conversation.

'Hello.' Charlie used her seductive voice. I strained to hear Mike's reply but his voice was just a low, sexy rumble.

'I'm terribly sorry, but Abigail's just slipped out. Is there something I can help you with?'

I imagined Charlie batting her eyelashes at Mike. It was a shame he was a cop. He was the first decent-looking bloke to show any kind of interest in me for ages, even if he did just want to slap me in handcuffs. Not that I'd mind playing cops and robbers with Mike, provided it was the right sort of game . . .

There was more rumbling and I crept nearer to the door to try to hear better.

'Perhaps you'd better come in, officer. We aren't in any kind of trouble, are we?'

Blood rushed in my ears as footsteps sounded

along the hall past my door and into the lounge. Charlie offered him a cup of tea, which he refused. They must have sat down then, as I heard the dodgy spring in our ancient sofa creaking.

'I have reason to believe you and your sister may be able to assist me with an inquiry, Miss Gifford. Abbey told me you were both acquainted with a Mr Freddie Davis?'

The palms of my hands were clammy as I pressed my ear to the door to hear Charlie's reply. I tried taking a peek through the gap but much to my frustration I couldn't see into the living room from my spying position.

'Oh yes, but we don't know him that well. He's more of a casual acquaintance.' Her voice was dismissive and cool. I'll say one thing for my sister, she's got nerves of steel. She'd always been bolder than me, better at taking risks.

'You have been seen with him on several occasions recently, both alone and in the company of your sister.' The sofa spring creaked again and I pictured Mike settling back on the seat, the little crinkles appearing at the corners of his eyes as he chatted.

'I'm not sure what you're implying, Mr . . . I'm sorry, what was your name again?' Charlie sounded positively glacial in response, and I was sneakily relieved that she wasn't responding to his charms.

'Flynn, Mike Flynn. I'm sorry, Miss Gifford, if you

feel I'm prying into your private affairs, but any information you can give me about Mr Davis and his movements may be pertinent to our investigations.'

I wiped my hands against the legs of my jeans. I could have done with using my inhaler but it was still in my handbag in the lounge. What did he mean? It sounded as if it was Freddie he was after rather than us.

'I'm afraid there's not much I can tell you. Mr Davis has taken me out for dinner a couple of times and he suggested a run out into the country for lunch the other day. I believe he was looking for a property investment but that's as much as I know.'

'I see. Well, thank you – are you going to be seeing him again?'

I heard the spring creak and guessed Charlie or Mike must have stood up. 'It's unlikely. Is Freddie aware that you're looking into his affairs?'

Mmm, good point. Score one to Charlie. I wasn't sure how ethical Mike's line of questioning was.

'Mr Davis and his barrister have been most co-operative.' The voices grew clearer and I guessed they must have come out of the lounge. I moved back from the gap. 'Should you hear from Mr Davis again, please let me know. Here's my card.' Mike's voice sounded very close now and I tried to control my breathing, which had become increasingly raspy with the stress of it all.

'Certainly, officer.'

The front door clicked open. 'Please tell Abbey I'm sorry I missed her.' His voice sounded crystal clear and a delicious quiver ran through my body. He must have known that I was still in the flat as he'd definitely locked eyes with me when he'd been out on the street earlier. I had a feeling that he knew I was standing right within earshot.

'Of course.'

The door snapped shut and I staggered gasping into the hall. 'Inhaler!'

'Bloody hell.' Charlie grabbed my handbag and threw it to me.

Kip emerged from his room, white-faced with distress as I took a couple of puffs and attempted to regain my breath.

'Now what?' My voice was still wheezy and my pulse galloped along with the steroid hit. If I kept having to take my medication at this rate I'd end up with bigger muscles than a female body builder.

Charlie's mobile phone started to ring. She picked it up from the table and looked at the screen.

'Freddie.' She clicked the button to take the call. 'Darling, you just caught me. I'm so sorry I had to dash yesterday. Honestly, my assistant is so bloody incompetent. She simply cannot cope in a crisis.' She raised an immaculately plucked eyebrow at me, and I stuck my tongue out at her before flopping down on the sofa. Kip took a seat next to me and I gave him a hug as we listened in to Charlie's conversation. She sounded the perfect society lady as she smooth-talked Freddie, pandering to his ego as if she was hanging on his every word.

'The solicitor will have the papers to you next week. I'll be out of the country for a few days, but it should all be ready for you to sign when I get back. Great-uncle Edward is quite keen to meet you so I said I'd arrange a little dinner party. Nothing fancy, just a few people.' She stopped talking and listened intently to Freddie's response.

'I'll look forward to it immensely. Be in touch soon. Bye.' She rolled her eyes at us and ended the call. 'That should buy us enough time to be out of here before he smells a rat – and no, I don't mean Claude.' She smiled at Kip. He didn't look very reassured.

The tightness in my chest had eased. 'It sounds as if Freddie may have been a naughty boy if the police are sniffing around him.'

'Maybe, but it's raised the heat round here all the same. I'm not happy with falling over Plod of the Yard every time we turn round.' Charlie drummed her fingernails on the tabletop. 'Time we moved north.'

It looked as if my new career in dog whispering was looming ever nearer. 'We need to fix up some accommodation.'

'Leave all that to me.' She whisked off to the

computer and perched herself in front of it. 'I've a lot of things lined up. I need to bring it all forward a touch, that's all.'

Kip still didn't look convinced. 'Will I be able to take Claude and Stig?'

Since most landlords weren't keen on tenants with pets, I wasn't certain how we would manage to house a rat and an iguana.

'No problem.' Charlie's fingers flew across the keyboard.

The next few days were a whirlwind of packing and organising. It was nothing new for us to be on the move since we were usually only a few paces ahead of the rent collector or the bailiffs. Kip always found the process unsettling however many times we did it, and the first bout of the regression therapy didn't appear to have helped me much either. Kip tried testing me in between sorting things out for the move.

'What am I holding?' He brandished a box of Coco Pops as we packed up the kitchen cupboards.

'Coco Pops.' I tried hard to say Shredded Wheat or cornflakes, but it was no use. The words stayed stuck in my brain. It was so frustrating I wanted to scream. How were we ever going to be able to pull off another job if I couldn't lie?

'What's this?' He waved an orange at me.

'An orange.' God, this was depressing. I'd desperately wanted to say apple.

'Are you sure you're trying, Abbey?' He stuffed the cereal in a box labelled 'Kitchen things'. I knew he was disappointed. He'd been convinced that he had the answer to my problems. In fairness, I'd been pretty convinced myself when I'd read the papers he'd printed off and the info that had accompanied the CD.

'Maybe I need more sessions.' I wasn't sure I *wanted* more sessions, but ever since the first one I'd found myself thinking about Mum more and more. I'd been four when she'd disappeared. Charlie had been thirteen and Kip just a baby. If my regression did hold some kind of clue to what had happened to her, then I had to find out more.

Kip frowned. 'You could be right. When we move to the new house we'll try again.'

I carried on placing crockery in the box. Charlie had arranged a visit to see Aunty Beatrice before we were to leave for Cheshire. Aunty Beatrice still had our birth certificates and some photographs of us as children. She also had a few pictures of Mum. None of us were looking forward to seeing the old misery again but as Charlie pointed out it was time we took the stuff back from her that was rightfully ours. While this sounded good in principle, I wasn't so sure it would work in practice.

*

'Moving again, Charlotte?'

We were sitting in a row on Aunty Beatrice's G-plan sofa, all holding dainty bone china cups full of insipid tea and wishing we were somewhere else. Memories of being told to wipe our feet, eat our sprouts and be seen and not heard were heavy in the air.

'It's work, Aunty Beatrice. Our company is quite successful but we do have to move where the jobs are.' Charlie gave Aunty Beatrice a tight little smile. I knew her memories of living here were the same as mine. It had been better than being in the children's care home, but not much better. My sister had borne the brunt of it all; she'd been a teenager when we'd moved in and had been turned into a mini-adult overnight. She'd been expected to do most of the household chores and care for Kip. Aunty Beatrice hadn't believed in letting Charlie go out with friends in case she fell into 'bad ways', like our mother. Later, as I'd got older, it had been my turn.

'I don't see why you need to drag poor Christopher with you. He knows he can always have a home with me.'

It took me a moment to realise she meant Kip. No one except Aunty Beatrice ever called him Christopher. The muscle in Kip's leg where it was pressed against mine tensed at the implied threat.

'That's very generous of you, Aunty, but we think a change of scenery might do him good.'

Aunty Beatrice surveyed him over the top of her teacup. 'He does look rather pasty,' she conceded. 'You're very quiet today, Abigail. Are you feeling well?'

I tried not to fidget as she turned her attention to me. 'Fine, thank you, Aunty.' We hadn't told her about the lightning strike. It would have been hard to explain the name and luckily the newspaper pictures had been of very poor quality.

'I've never really understood exactly what kind of business you could possibly be in that necessitates all this flitting around.'

Luckily Charlie jumped in before my runaway mouth could confess the truth and give Aunty Beatrice heart failure.

'It's marketing and promotions. We supply services to businesses and individuals. Moving to Cheshire is a wonderful opportunity for us all.'

I suppose that was one way of describing what we did.

Aunty Beatrice didn't appear impressed. 'It seems very fly-by-night to me.'

We continued to sit in an uncomfortable silence sipping our tea. The wooden-cased clock on the mantelpiece ticked away the minutes.

'We were wondering, Aunty, if you still had the box with our birth certificates and the papers about Mum.' Charlie put her cup down on its saucer and placed it on the coffee table.

Aunty Beatrice frowned. 'Of course I have. There isn't much in it. Why the sudden interest in those mouldy old papers?'

'We'd really like to have it ourselves, if you wouldn't mind, now that Abbey and Kip are older,' Charlie forged on.

The crease across Aunty Beatrice's forehead deepened. 'Well, I suppose you can take the box if that's what you want, but it is perfectly safe here, you know.' She got up from her armchair and headed off upstairs to retrieve the box, presumably from its usual resting place on the top of her wardrobe.

'Phew, that went better than I thought,' I whispered to Charlie as soon as the old battleaxe was out of earshot.

'She won't make me stay here, will she?' Kip muttered, casting his gaze around Aunty Beatrice's neat and tidy lounge. His fingers beat an anxious tattoo on the hand-crocheted cover on the arm of the sofa.

I gave his hand a squeeze. 'Don't be silly. You know we'd never go anywhere without you.'

The stairs squeaked so we stopped talking and sat up straighter on the sofa. Aunty Beatrice shuffled back into the room carrying the large square cardboard box that contained the entire history of our family. She set it down on the coffee table before resuming her position on the armchair.

'I'm entrusting this to you, Charlotte, as you're the eldest.' Her tone implied that she was about to bestow some priceless treasure upon us.

'I'll take good care of everything,' Charlie promised.

'There's nothing of any monetary value. Your mother was always feckless.'

'Do you ever wonder what happened to her, Aunty Beatrice?' I don't know what possessed me to speak. I don't think any of us had ever dared voice that particular question to her before. Kip bumped my ankle with his foot to tell me to shut up.

To my surprise my aunt's gimlet eyes grew misty. 'I don't know, Abigail. I expect she met a bad end.' Her shoulders stiffened and she gave a sniff. 'Lally was always looking for the good life. I warned her it would end in tears.'

Charlie glared at me and I put down my cup.

'We'd better be off then, Aunty. We'll be in touch once we've settled in our new place.' Charlie nudged me and Kip picked up the box, ready to leave.

'You will be careful, won't you, Charlotte?' Aunty Beatrice followed us into the magnolia-painted woodchip-papered hallway.

'Of course,' Charlie reassured her. 'I'm always careful when I'm driving.'

Ha. That was a fib for a start. Charlie was a terrible driver.

Aunty Beatrice bit her lip. 'I didn't mean with

your journey. I meant be careful with the contents of that box. Your mother's gone; let it rest.'

We all stared at her.

'Christopher's a sensitive boy. It doesn't do to go raking over the past.'

'The police have already been through these papers a million times,' Charlie said. 'I don't expect there's anything very startling in there.'

'Well, just be careful, that's all. Some things are best left alone.' It sounded almost as if she was back-pedalling – as if she'd said too much.

Charlie unlatched the front door. She and Kip walked down the path to the van.

'We will be careful, Aunty.' On an impulse I bent and kissed her cheek. Her skin felt dry and powdery against my lips and I could smell her Estee Lauder perfume. She suddenly looked frail and old, standing by the open door. I had a feeling she knew we planned to go poking around and she was afraid.

'Good luck, Abigail.'

I wished I knew what she was afraid of.

We were due to depart for pastures new the next day. We always travelled light, renting the furniture in our various flats and houses. The remainder of our worldly possessions – clothes, kitchen stuff, pets, and so on – would fit in the van. It made for a cramped journey, but as we usually didn't move very far it had never been a problem.

This journey would be somewhat longer, however, and it would have been nice to hire a bigger van for the move. But the new job would require a higher initial investment so we'd gone for the budget option. Charlie's mobile rang as we finished breakfast.

'Damn, it's Freddie. What does he want?' She answered the call as Kip and I tidied the last remaining pieces of crockery into a box and washed up. We heard the tirade of abuse from the other side of the kitchen. Charlie listened for a few seconds then clicked the phone off and dropped it into the empty cutlery drawer.

'The jig's up.' Her hands shook as she slammed the drawer shut.

'What's happened? I thought we'd have a few more days before he caught on.' Unless someone had tipped him off . . . My prime suspect was Mike Flynn. Maybe he was a bent copper. The thought didn't appeal. There was nothing worse than a bent policeman.

'We would have, except the real Lady Charlotte Bloom has got herself arrested for being drunk and disorderly on the flight home from South Africa. Apparently it's all over the TV and the papers, complete with her picture.' Charlie blew out a breath. 'She tried to shag some bit-part soap actor in the aeroplane loo.'

'Oh.' I sat down with a bump. Guiltily, I felt a rush of relief that it hadn't been Mike who'd dropped us in it. I didn't want him to be to blame. He might be the enemy but I didn't want to believe the worst of him.

'Good job we're moving today.' Her complexion had paled and I didn't think she was as calm as she was making out.

'Freddie sounded nasty.' Kip blinked at us.

'Well, he was never going to be happy about losing thirty thousand pounds, but he made some very violent threats. You heard him.' Charlie fiddled with the edge of a tea towel before folding it and dropping it in the packing box.

I placed the last of the kitchen things on top of the towel. 'Lucky we're moving away, then. The heat will have died down by the time we come back and there's not much chance of him finding us in Cheshire.'

'But he said he'd track us down.' Kip was fretting.

'He doesn't know our last names or where we are. Everything will be fine.' I tried to sound confident so he wouldn't worry. He looked relieved, so I must have been convincing. I just hoped Freddie wouldn't come looking for us. The threats to make us pay had sounded as if it wasn't only money-focused revenge that he planned to exact. It would have been a huge blow to his self-esteem to discover he'd been conned by two girls.

With the last of the boxes in the van the only remaining task was to transfer Stig the iguana and Claude the rat into their travelling boxes and pack them at the back. Charlie refused to have anything to do with moving Kip's animals so she settled down on the freshly scrubbed couch with the map to recheck our route. I got lumbered with Claude while Kip ensured Stig would be comfortable on the journey.

I had my head inside the van, rearranging stuff around Claude's cage, when a male voice that was becoming all too familiar sounded behind me.

'Going somewhere, Abbey?'

I whirled round so quickly I bumped my head on the side of the van. Mike leaned against a lamppost, his dark brown eyes quizzical as he took in all our belongings. God, but the man was gorgeous, broad-shouldered and long-limbed and exuding that air of mystery which just got me every time we met.

'Um, we're moving.' I looked around for Charlie or Kip but they were nowhere in sight.

'Oh? Going far?' He was way too sexy to be a cop. He also had the effect of sending my insides to mush every time I was near him.

'Near Wilmslow, Cheshire,' I squeaked. This telling-the-truth business was killing me. If he asked me where exactly I'd have no choice but to give him the full bit, even down to the postcode! 'What brings you here?' I decided to turn the tables. He kept popping up like a bad penny and if he was after Freddie then why did he keep hounding us? I wasn't vain enough to believe he was interested in me for other, more personal reasons . . . although it would have been nice if he was.

'I heard a rumour that concerned me.' His dark eyes were fixed on my face and I felt the heat creeping up my cheeks.

'Oh?' Where the hell was Charlie?

'Freddie Davis is not a very nice man. He's not a good man to cross.'

A shiver ran down my spine. 'Really?' My tongue stuck to the roof of my mouth. I could smell the woody notes of his cologne. I had been right: it was professional not personal business that had brought him here. My heart did a mini-plummet towards my trainers.

Even so . . .

'I don't know the precise nature of you and your sister's connection to Freddie, but my advice would be to stay well away from him.' Mike straightened and took a step towards me. The toes of his shoes were almost touching mine. Electricity seemed to crackle in the space between us.

I swallowed. 'Cheshire is pretty far.'

'Be very careful, Abbey. I'll see you around.' He gave me that same intent look he'd given me earlier, then slowly bent his head until his lips brushed mine. My eyes closed as I tasted testosterone, coffee and a dangerously sexy man.

When I opened my eyes he was gone. Poof! As if he'd never been there. I was left standing like a dummy in the middle of the street. I looked around, but he'd vanished and I didn't want to be too obvious in case he was watching me from nearby and laughing at me. I barely knew the man – what the hell had just happened?

Charlie and Kip emerged from the entrance to the flats carrying Stig's cage between them and bickering over why Kip had pets in the first place. I grabbed the sleeve of Charlie's jacket and pulled her to one side while Kip made sure the cage was firmly wedged.

'Mike was just here,' I hissed, keeping my voice low so Kip wouldn't overhear.

Charlie looked around. 'Policeman Mike? What was he doing here again?'

'Warning us about Freddie and his bad temper.'

Charlie frowned. 'He's sweet on you. God, Abbey.' She raked her hand through her long black hair. 'I suppose you told him we were moving?'

'Yes, but come on, it was pretty obvious with the van loaded to the hilt and all.' I decided to keep the kiss to myself. After all, she wasn't likely to ask if he'd kissed me, so it was at least one secret I would be able to keep.

She stomped round to the driver's door. 'You didn't give him the address as well, did you?'

'No.'

But only because he hadn't asked for it. In a way that was depressing because, despite his kissing me, it meant he wasn't keen to see me again. Wow, how confusing was that? I mean, it wouldn't be any good seeing him again anyway. He'd ask me questions, I'd blurt out answers, and instead of a romantic candlelit dinner for two it would be a cell at the local nick.

Charlie stared at me. 'Abbey?'

She'd obviously been talking to me and I'd missed it. The back door of the van slammed shut and Kip sauntered round to join us.

'Stig and Claude are in. Are we going now?'

I climbed in the front passenger seat. It was only as I buckled my seatbelt that I realised Mike had said 'see you around'. Something else that would be best not shared with Charlie.

'When we've unloaded at the new house I'll trade

the van in,' she announced, steering us from the middle lane into the fast lane of the motorway at breakneck speed. 'Now your new policeman friend has the details we're too traceable.'

'I like the van,' Kip protested through a mouthful of Haribo.

'We can't take chances. Besides, this new job means I need to project a certain image so we'll need a car to reflect that.' She leaned on the horn as a van in the middle lane suddenly pulled out in front of us.

'What sort of car?' I prayed she didn't mean a sports car. She was doing her best to kill us in a van so she'd be deadly in anything designed for speed.

'Something very respectable, but a little fun,' she pronounced and grabbed some of Kip's Haribo to pop in her mouth. I closed my eyes and prayed she'd keep both hands on the wheel.

'Do you want me to research some cars?' Kip offered eagerly. Like most teenage boys he loved cars. He could quote fuel consumption, nought-to-sixty times, and paint options for virtually every model on the market.

'I need something that suggests I'm a respectable, hard-working Catholic secretary.' Charlie snagged another Haribo and the van swerved dangerously.

I stifled a giggle. 'What car can do all that?'

'There are several possibilities.' Kip slurped on a fizzy cola-bottle sweet. 'I can come to the car auctions with you.'

This was a big offer – he hated being in crowds or noise.

'When are you going to tell us more details about this job, anyway?' I picked out a funny sherbet sweet from the bag. Charlie never let on much about the scams until she'd worked out all the details. However, since she'd uprooted us and dragged us halfway up the country I thought she could have been a bit more forthcoming.

'All in good time.' She grinned and turned on the radio, putting an end to any further questions.

The traffic grew busier the nearer we got to Manchester and I was relieved when we finally left the motorway to head for the suburbs. Charlie had somehow managed to rent us a fully furnished house in what looked like a very nice area. It would be strange to live in a house that was all ours and not divided into flats. Kip was wildly excited at the prospect of a garden.

We stopped off at the letting agents so Charlie could sign the papers and collect the keys. I desperately wanted to see the house. I'd seen it on the website, but it would be good to finally get in and unpack. It looked like a giant improvement on our London flat. Not that the flat had been bad, but I'd always wanted to live in a real house with stairs and everything.

Maybe Kip and I were more alike than I'd realised. I guess deep inside I'd always wanted a regular life, just like him. A nice, safe suburban life in a bog-standard nineteen-thirties semi with a mum and dad, a cat, and a lovely, boring office job someplace where the staff went to the pub on Fridays after work. In other words – normality. It would be nice to be able to stay in one place more than a few months. Perhaps living here we would be like everyone else. We wouldn't be the people whose mother had disappeared or the girls with the weird kid brother. We could be Charlie, Abbey and Kip, living a normal life in a normal house doing normal things like other people. Other *normal* people.

We pulled up outside a fairly modern semi at the head of a quiet cul-de-sac. Kip leaned forward from his seat behind me and Charlie. 'Is this it?'

'Home sweet home.' Charlie yanked up the handbrake and turned off the ignition.

We sat for a moment looking at our new house. I had a lump in my throat for some stupid reason.

'Well, let's check it out then.' Charlie jingled the keys.

Kip had the door of the van open before I'd even managed to undo my seatbelt. I followed him and Charlie along the neat row of paving slabs that led to the front door. It was ludicrous to feel so excited. We'd moved so many times and lived in so many places since Mum had disappeared, it was stupid to think of this house as a home. Yet I couldn't shake off that 'kid at Christmas' feeling as Charlie opened the front door.

The inside of the house was beautiful. Clean and light with lovely furniture. A welcome bouquet of flowers stood on the mantelpiece in a pretty crystal vase next to a bottle of wine and a card.

'Are you okay?' Charlie slipped her arm round me and gave me a hug. I nodded. Kip had headed out to the small conservatory at the rear of the lounge to look at the garden.

'It's lovely, isn't it?' She smiled, but there was the glitter of tears on her long dark lashes. I had never thought my sister might share my and Kip's desire for a home but it looked as though I'd misjudged her.

Charlie had spent so long being the tough, practical one, I'd forgotten she was as vulnerable and damaged by our childhood as Kip and I were. She had probably suffered more as she'd been older and hadn't been able to share her fears; instead, she'd been the one who'd had to listen to me and Kip.

'Yeah.' I hugged her back.

'Abbey, Charlie, come and see!'

Kip's face was alight with excitement. We stood next to him and admired the garden together. Silver birch trees waved in the late afternoon breeze at the far end of the lawn. Borders of flowers and shrubs spilled on to the grass, tangled and colourful in the sunlight.

'Isn't this great? I can make a bird table,' Kip breathed.

'We'd better unpack,' Charlie suggested.

'I'll get Claude and Stig!' He whirled round and hurried back out to the van, leaving us to go and inspect the bedrooms.

Charlie bagged the master bedroom with en suite. Kip took the small room next to hers, as we decided he could have the conservatory for his model-making. That left me with the second biggest bedroom overlooking the garden. My room at the old flat had overlooked the bins from a Chinese restaurant. This was a vast improvement. I could hear Charlie bossing Kip around downstairs as he carried in the boxes. I sat on the end of my new bed and admired the view. No more grimy bricks or stinky bins, just the gentle rustle of green leaves.

We celebrated our move with a fish and chip supper and the bottle of wine the letting agents had left for us. It seemed very quiet without the familiar roar of traffic outside or the dull thump of someone else's stereo. We sprawled about the lounge with our plates and glasses as we unwound after the journey.

'I'll trade in the van in the morning. Kip, you need to get us set up on the Internet. Abbey, enrol us at the library and suss out the locality.' Charlie poured some more wine into her glass and took a generous mouthful.

'Okay, then what?' Tomorrow was Saturday. With

any luck we would get Sunday off to do a spot of sunbathing in our new garden. I'd spotted the perfect place to put a lounger.

'Sunday we go to Mass and introduce ourselves to our new parish priest.'

'Why church?' I didn't think Charlie had found religion.

'It's important for the job. Our next mark and his family will be there.'

My spirits sank a little as Charlie elaborated a little on her scam. It looked as if my sunbathing plans were scuppered. Kip paused in the act of feeding batter scraps to Claude. 'Are we Catholic? I don't think we ought to fib to God.'

'We *are* Catholic, as it happens,' Charlie explained. 'Well, Mum and Aunty Beatrice are.'

At the mention of Mum we all looked at the box we'd collected from Aunty Beatrice's. When we'd carried our meagre belongings into the house Kip had stashed it in the corner of the lounge. It sat in the corner, still sealed.

'We should have a look at what's in it.' Part of me wanted to see if there was anything that would explain my weird regression experience, yet part of me didn't. Perhaps Aunty Beatrice's nervousness had rubbed off on me. Or perhaps it was because it might mean letting go of my childish dream that someday my mother would reappear in our lives and we would be a family again.

'I don't think it'll hold many surprises.' Charlie took another glug of wine. I sensed that the idea of opening the box had unsettled her as much as me.

'We should go through everything, though. There might be something there, something that was missed by the police. You see it all the time in films.' Kip finished feeding Claude and wiped his greasy hands on the legs of his jeans.

'Hey, I don't think it's going to be like CSI.' I didn't want him getting overexcited thinking he was about to turn into Sherlock Holmes or Hercule Poirot.

Charlie uncurled herself from the cream leather armchair and moved the box to the coffee table so we could all see the contents.

'Okay, here goes.' She blew the remainder of the light layer of dust from the lid and opened it up.

7

Kip leaned forward, breathing heavily through his mouth, as Charlie lifted out the contents of the box. On top of the pile were our birth certificates. We'd seen those before; all of them had the space for 'father' left blank. Since we didn't look alike, and given Aunty Beatrice's stern disapproval, we'd always suspected we had different fathers.

Charlie was dark with faintly Oriental features and green eyes, while Kip had milk-white skin, red hair and blue eyes. I suppose out of the three of us I was the one who most resembled Mum, and even then it wasn't that much of a likeness. Sadly, the person I most resembled was a younger version of Aunty Beatrice.

We'd asked Aunty Beatrice a couple of times but she couldn't or wouldn't tell us anything. Charlie remembered Mum dating but her recollections were hazy and she didn't remember many men coming back to the flat. Since we had so little to go on the subject of our paternity was an unanswered question. No one except Aunty Beatrice had come forward when Mum had disappeared and there had been an appeal for relatives, so it seemed safe to assume that whoever our fathers were they hadn't wanted to stick around.

Then there was Mum's birth certificate: Eulalie Frances Rosemary Gifford. Her passport was there too, long since expired. There were a few pictures of Aunty Beatrice and Mum when they were younger – wearing white dresses and gloves for their confirmation, in bathing costumes on the beach and playing on a seesaw in jeans. Then it was a fast-forward through time to Mum looking glam and pretty with an eighties hairdo and big shoulder pads, and Aunty Beatrice wearing a dress with a Lady Di collar and a hat with a little net veil.

Kip moved the photographs to one side to reveal a pile of yellowing press cuttings. We took turns to read the media coverage of our mother's dis-appearance. *Three children found abandoned in deserted flat*. The various journalists' disapproval of our mother's lifestyle appeared to match Aunty Beatrice's. No one, it seemed, had come forward to say they had seen Mum. She had stepped out of our flat that evening seventeen years ago and vanished.

'Nothing.' Charlie frowned as she finally dropped the last cutting on to the pile.

'Is there anything else in the box?' Kip folded back the lid and lifted out a smaller container. It looked like an old-fashioned tea caddy, a tin painted in black and gold with a picture of a Japanese woman twirling a parasol on the side. 'What's in here?'

'Mum's jewellery, I think,' Charlie said.

Kip opened the lid and tipped out the contents. Several pairs of cheap earrings, a couple of brooches and a necklace fell on to the coffee table.

'There's something stuck to the side.' Kip peered inside the tin, squinting as he prised out a stiff and dirty piece of card that had been jammed tight against the wall of the tin. 'It's just an old party invitation.' He threw it down in disgust.

Charlie picked it up. 'It must have been important. This was Mum's treasure tin. She only ever kept things she thought were valuable or special in it.'

I leaned across her so I could read it. 'What date did Mum leave?'

Kip rummaged in the cuttings to check. 'The same Saturday as the event on this invitation.'

'But there's no mention of her going out to a party in any of the papers.' I looked through them all again just to check. 'That would have been why she was dressed up in her best shoes and I smelt perfume. That is, if my dream is about the night Mum vanished.' I plucked the card from Charlie's grasp.

'It was the same night, I know it was. I remember her getting ready to go out. Surely the police would have known about this? They would have spoken to everyone at the party to find out if they'd seen her.'

Even as she spoke I could see Charlie wasn't certain.

'The card was in the tin. Maybe she didn't go,' Kip suggested.

Charlie shook her head. 'No, if it was important enough for Mum to have put this in her treasure tin she must have intended to go. And I watched her get dressed. She said she'd be back after midnight and not to open the door to anyone.'

'Should we go to the police?' I knew it was a stupid thing to say. It had been seventeen years and all we could show them was an old and tatty invitation to an event our mother might not even have attended.

'We should do some investigating ourselves first. See if we can find something out on our own before we take it to the police.' Kip took the card from me as if certain he could extract hidden information from the neatly engraved print.

'The party was at a nightclub. There could have been hundreds of people there.' I started to stack up the photographs. More pictures of Mum laughing happily among various groups of people. A couple of them looked as if they had been taken at a wedding. In one she wore a pencil skirt with a ruffled blouse and a cross-looking dark-haired little girl was clutching her hand.

'Here's one of you, Charlie.' I passed it over for her to see.

'Very flattering.' She flipped her hair behind

her shoulder and studied the picture. 'Who's this in the background? Behind me and Mum, in that group?'

I moved closer so I could see. The man was slightly out of focus, but she was right – there was something familiar about him.

'It's Freddie!' We both spoke at the same time.

Kip grabbed the corner of the picture to bring it nearer to him. 'Are you sure?'

'Look at the bracelet, and the way he's standing.' Charlie tweaked it back again.

'Freddie knew Mum?' I felt a bit dazed. Terrific – the one lead we had into our past and it was the man who would most likely kill us if he ever caught up with us.

Charlie released the photograph, allowing Kip to pore over the image. 'Mum did know a lot of people. That picture looks as if it might have been taken at a wedding or a christening. Anyway, I was almost thirteen when she left and how old am I there? Six or seven, maybe?'

We took turns to scrutinise the rest of the snaps in the hope that we might find something else of interest, but nothing obvious leapt out at us.

'We could ask Aunty Beatrice. I mean, they were still close after she had you. It was only later when I was born that she disowned Mum.' Even as I spoke I had my doubts about what I was suggesting. Perhaps this was the veiled warning that Aunty

Beatrice had given me when we'd last seen her.

'I don't know.' Charlie sounded dubious. 'Let's see if Kip turns anything up on the party invitation first.'

'I'll do some searching on the Net when I get us hooked up.' Kip's enthusiasm, as ever, was undiminished.

We packed everything back in the box, but Charlie kept the photograph of her and Mum. She planned to get a frame so she could display it in the lounge. I wished there had been some of me and Kip with Mum too, but there weren't. The only childhood pictures of us were the ones social services had taken before they had managed to raise Aunty Beatrice.

I remembered the day those pictures had been taken. I'd been really excited because I'd been wearing a new pink dress and had big white ribbon bows on my pigtails. We were lined up on a bench seat with me in the middle holding on tight to Kip. Charlie wasn't smiling in the photo. The social worker who had been supervising the session had made her take off her blue eyeshadow, so she had sulked.

Our picture had been in some publicity shots to try to trace any relatives or to place us with an adoptive family. That was when Aunty Beatrice had reappeared in our lives and we had moved from the children's home to her house.

'I'm turning in. We've a busy weekend ahead.'

Charlie yawned, stretching her arms up above her head.

I tidied up the mess from our supper and turned out the lights. Upstairs in my new bedroom I snuggled under the quilt and looked at the photo of us as children in the pastel light from my mood lamp. Kip had been a very sweet baby. As I shut off the light I wondered what had happened to our mother. Much as I longed for her to return, in my heart I knew it had to be something bad.

Kip was up bright and early the next morning. I could hear him thumping about downstairs, whistling a tuneless refrain over and over again as he clomped around. A quick squint at the alarm clock told me it was still o'dark o'clock. Unfortunately, the birds outside my window seemed to be in collusion with Kip and were busy chirping their noisy beaks off. I gave in to the inevitable and stumbled downstairs for a cup of tea.

'Hi, Abbey. You're up early.'

Bits of cable and corrugated cardboard packing material lay strewn across the lounge floor. I crossed my fingers behind my back and prayed he was installing the computer and not taking another of our appliances to bits.

'I wanted a cup of tea. Can I get you one?'

'Yes, please.' He jumped up from the floor and sat down in front of the screen.

'And some Coco Pops?' Thank goodness he appeared to be doing what Charlie wanted.

He nodded as he concentrated on whatever it was he was looking for.

I trudged off in search of the cup that cheers and some breakfast.

'Yes!'

His triumphal shout made me spill Coco Pops all over the kitchen worktop.

'Found some unprotected wireless networks we can use,' he explained as I slid a bowl of his favourite cereal next to his elbow. 'Otherwise it'll take ages to get broadband.'

'Whatever.' Before my first hit of tea I had no clue what he was on about.

Charlie had done a shedload of research on the area before renting the house. Folders stuffed with maps and information were heaped in a box at the end of the sofa. I took a slurp from my mug and pulled out the map showing me where the library and supermarkets were situated.

'What kind of car do you think Charlie will get?' Kip had found the Ferrari site on the Net and was whizzing the cursor over the stockists' details. There appeared to be a dealership not too far away.

'No idea. It sounded as if she had something specific in mind, though.' I didn't think it was likely to be a sports car from her description yesterday.

Actually, I had no idea what make of car could possibly fit the bill for what she wanted.

Kip twizzled round in his seat to face me. 'Why does Charlie want us to go to church?'

'The new mark, Philippe, lives with his family and they're all very devout Catholics. His mother vets all his girlfriends and she doesn't approve of the nightclub set. Charlie has plans to engineer a series of innocent meetings with him and his family at church and the supermarket and stuff. She wants to figure out a way to get close to them.' Charlie had given me some details but not as many as I would have liked.

Kip stirred his Coco Pops round in the bowl. I watched the milk turn brown while he thought about Charlie's plan. 'So, what about the dogs?'

'They have two neurotic dogs which Philippe adores. They also keep a huge stash of money and gold jewellery in the safe at the house. I think the dog plan might be in case he doesn't fall for Charlie. She needs someone to get inside to case the joint.' I'd tried to forget about the dogs. Unlike Kip, I'm not that big an animal lover – especially when the animals in question have large teeth. My memories of my encounter with the police dog were still a bit too vivid.

Charlie strolled into the lounge, yawning and clutching her hair straighteners. 'What are you two doing?'

'Net's up.' Kip waved his hand in the direction of the computer screen.

'Kettle's hot.' I took another sip of my tea as Charlie flopped down next to me on the sofa.

'Great.'

I took that as my cue to get her a drink.

'By the way, I've a job interview on Monday.' She started to straighten her hair as I placed her drink on the table.

'Job interview?' Kip and I spoke together. The idea of paid work and Charlie lumped together was an alien concept. She hadn't had a 'proper' job since she'd quit her beautician's course. Working nine to five in an office wasn't really her; plus, of course, we'd needed the money. She loved the buzz she got from pulling off a successful scam and the adrenalin rush that came from taking risks. Sometimes this aspect of her personality worried me a bit.

'Secretary, working for a local charity.' She frowned at us from under her fringe. 'Philippe's mother, Bella, is the main patron.'

Kip raised his eyebrows and his shoulders. 'How are you going to get to be a secretary?'

'Trust me – the job is mine.' She smiled and continued to smooth her hair into its usual shining black waterfall.

I finished my tea. Charlie hadn't confided all the details in me the way she normally did when she was planning a scam. I knew, at least, that we weren't using false names this time. Usually she'd have gone over every minor detail with me by now; immaculate planning was her trademark. This time, however, she'd just gone over the very basics and it felt surprisingly hurtful to be out of the loop. But then again, after what I'd blurted out already, I could guess why she wasn't telling me everything.

It was strange. Not being able to lie any more was causing me problems, yet I would have sworn that as a family we had always been honest with one another. It shows how wrong you could be, I suppose, as it was becoming obvious that all of us had our little secrets.

Charlie took the van off to trade in and Kip settled down to surf the Net for clues to the invitation we'd found in Mum's treasure tin. I'd worked out from the map where the library was and decided to go there first. The groceries could come later. I didn't fancy hauling a load of bags home so I figured I could get a cab as it wasn't too far from our new house to Sainsbury's.

There seemed no point in glamming up, so I scraped my hair back into a ponytail and pulled on an old pair of trackie bottoms and a T-shirt. Big mistake.

The library wasn't so bad although the librarian, a Mr Biggs, didn't seem quite as helpful as Sanjay, the chap who'd run our previous one. Sainsbury's was a different matter entirely. The car park had plenty of gleaming Mercs and BMWs alongside the inevitable

4×4s. Either this was a much more affluent area than I'd expected or Cheshire women took much more care over their appearance and than I did. I trolled around the shelves feeling even more scruffy and invisible than usual.

If I'd been concentrating I wouldn't have done it. Strange supermarkets take a lot of effort as you don't know where everything is, so I was busy scouring the shelves for Kip's favourite chocolate spread when I trod on Philippe.

Literally.

Number one, it's not good to meet your mark before the scam gets under way, and number two, standing on a Premiership footballer's toes is never a good move – ever.

It wouldn't have occurred to me that he'd be in a supermarket doing the shopping on a Saturday anyway. I mean, shouldn't he have been running round after a ball somewhere?

'Oh, I'm so sorry.' My face felt the same colour as the tomatoes he had in his wire basket.

'It's okay.' He had a very nice smile and just the faintest hint of an accent. When I'd seen the pic Charlie had of him from the Net I hadn't realised he was so nice looking. His skin was a lovely golden-brown, the sort that's natural and not from a sunbed. He looked nicely muscular and had very gorgeous dark eyes. I'd have to find out more info from Charlie on his background. He carried on looking at me with a polite expression on his face until I realised I was blocking his way.

'Sorry.' I dived to the side so he could get past me. Unfortunately, he moved the same way so we ended up doing an awkward jig in the preserves aisle. If the ground had opened up and swallowed me it would have done me a favour.

Once he'd escaped I headed for the freezer cabinets to cool myself down. Opening one of the doors and sticking my nose next to the tubs of Häagen Dazs was probably the only way I'd regain enough composure to be able to face him again.

With any luck, when we met tomorrow at church he wouldn't recognise me. People didn't tend to remember me, which was why I was so good at conning them. This encounter had been a bit different, though, because I'd been me, and not disguised. Instead of blending into the background and being forgettable the way I normally was, I stood out amongst the smart shoppers of Sainsbury's like a mongrel at Crufts.

It would be nice to meet people as me. Not how I'd just met Philippe, but just to be able to relax and not have to think about my character or back-story. It would be nice to have friends. Charlie, Kip and I didn't have friends. It was too tricky when you were always pretending to be someone else, the way Charlie and I were. Kip didn't like meeting people. Left to himself he would have been a hermit, living alone on a remote island somewhere with his animals.

At least he *had* his animals. Charlie and I just had each other.

I paid the taxi fare outside the house on my return from the supermarket. The driver helped me unload the groceries and left me outside the front door with a pile of bulging carrier bags. It wouldn't be worth ringing the bell for Kip to come and carry some of the bags into the house for me. He would just bolt for his room and hide the moment he heard the noise.

The key had worked its way to the bottom of my bag so it took me a minute to wriggle it free and get everything inside.

'Kip, I'm back.' I carried the shopping through to the kitchen.

The house was quiet. The computer was still on, showing the screen saver, and I wondered where he'd gone. Once everything was unpacked I switched on the kettle then went to look for him.

His room was empty. Stig blinked sleepily at me from his tank in the conservatory and Claude twitched his whiskers enquiringly as I called Kip's name. The heat had built up in the house so I opened the kitchen window to let in some air. Then I noticed the back door was unlocked. As I stepped out into the garden I heard the murmur of voices.

Kip's flame-red hair stood out against the dark green of the conifers that separated our garden from next door.

'Hello, Abbey. I didn't hear you come back.' He jumped down from his perch on the edge of an oblong stone garden trough filled with pink bedding plants.

'I thought I heard voices.'

His face flushed dark crimson. 'I was, um, just talking to Sophie.'

'Sophie?' I looked in the direction of the fence but couldn't see anything, or anyone.

'She lives next door,' Kip mumbled.

'Oh.' It was hard to keep the surprise out of my voice. He never spoke to anyone except me or Charlie unless it was a dire emergency or we were on a job and he was forced into it.

'She seems really nice. She's got a rabbit and a cat.'

'Oh.' I followed him into the kitchen. 'How did you meet her?' It would have been interesting to have seen the mysterious Sophie.

'Her rabbit got through the fence.' He pulled a couple of mugs from the cupboard and switched the kettle back on.

I leaned back against the sink unit and studied his

face as I waited for the rest of the story. 'What's she like?'

'Really cute with long ears and a wiggly nose.'

I hit him with the tea towel. 'I meant what is *Sophie* like, not the rabbit.'

Kip frowned as if he hadn't thought much about the matter. 'Nice.'

It didn't sound as if I would get much more from him. I'd have to look out for this Sophie myself if I wanted to know more about her.

The sound of a car door closing got our attention. I raced Kip to the front door, eager to see what car Charlie had bought.

'It's a Golf.' Kip pushed past me to examine the bright blue paintwork of our new family transport.

'It's perfect for the job.' Charlie jingled the keys. 'We need to handle Philippe and his family very carefully. I don't want anything messing it up.'

I didn't think it would be a good idea to tell her about meeting him in the supermarket. I had a feeling that little incident might come under the 'stuffing things up' heading.

We were all up bright and early next morning ready for the Gifford family outing to Mass. Charlie and I looked very demure in our best suits. Mine was grey and hers was black. Kip had to be bribed into smart jeans and a casual jacket with the promise of a McDonald's drive-thru meal if he went with us.

'What's the plan for today?' I buckled my belt as Kip levered his long legs into the back seat.

'Today we're scoping everything out. If I can catch Philippe's eye that would be excellent. I have my interview tomorrow for the charity job and then we need to work on gaining access to the property. That's where you'll come in with the dog training.' Charlie crunched the gears as she swung the Golf out of our quiet street into the busier main road.

'Um, about that ... I don't know that dogs are really the right area for me.' I had been hoping she might drop the pet psychology idea.

'Just because you were bitten by an Alsatian once doesn't mean you can't handle Philippe's dogs. It's only a ploy so you can get a crack at the safe and a look at the alarm.' Unperturbed by my protest, she cut in front of a Jag at the traffic lights before diving across into the church car park and slotting the Golf into a vacant space.

'Supposing I get asked something?'

Charlie frowned at me. 'Such as? I've thought of that. You aren't likely to be asked anything that could possibly give away the plan. At worst if you say something inappropriate they'll just think you're a bit batty.'

Kip and I trailed after Charlie as she strutted up the steps and into the church, dutifully crossing herself as she stepped inside.

'I don't like this,' Kip muttered as we each

accepted a hymn book and filed into a pew.

'Me either.' We all bowed our heads for a moment in contemplation. I half expected another bolt of lightning to descend and strike me down like the one that had hit me outside Debenhams.

'There's Philippe and his family,' Charlie whispered.

A petite woman with grey-streaked dark hair strode past us on dangerously high heels. She was followed by a small, skinny girl of about ten wearing a very stiff lace-trimmed dress and ankle socks, then Philippe, dark-eyed and good looking in his designer suit.

I noticed Charlie, who was seated on the end of the pew nearest the aisle, cross her legs as Philippe drew near. Only the flicker of his eyelashes betrayed his interest in her long calves encased in sheer black nylon. He took a seat next to his sister and after a moment gave a seemingly casual glance back in our direction. Thankfully his attention was on Charlie and he showed no sign of recognising me.

The service seemed to drone on for ever, with Charlie nudging us into standing and sitting at the right moments. We mouthed our way through the hymns and prayers, Kip fidgeting and sweating from the nerves of being amongst so many people. Finally it was over and everyone stood up ready to make their way out of the building.

Charlie timed her exit from our pew so that she

stepped out into the aisle right in front of Philippe.

'Good morning.' He had a nice smile. I hadn't taken too much notice at the supermarket but he *really* was a good-looking guy.

'Hello.' My sister smiled back and I knew his charm wasn't lost on her. In fact, he was just Charlie's type. He was definitely a more attractive prospect for a date than Freddie.

Philippe's mother bustled past me and Kip in order to walk next to her son. I guessed she was checking out Charlie by the way she cut her eyes at us as she went past.

We paused on the steps to shake hands with the priest and make polite conversation, then I walked away with Kip. He'd had enough by now and needed to go somewhere quiet, so we returned to the car. Charlie stayed to chat for a few more minutes and I guessed she had taken the opportunity to ingratiate herself with Philippe and his mum.

'Result!' She beamed as she sat down in the driver's seat and took the keys from me.

'Can we get a burger now?' Kip asked.

'And a milkshake.' Charlie started the car and we sailed off to find McDonald's.

'I take it everything went well?' I tried not to flinch at her last-minute braking as we tagged on to the end of the queue for the drive-thru.

'Marvellously – like a dream. I spoke to Philippe's mother, only a few words, nothing too much. He seemed quite interested in me.' She smiled and admired her manicure as we waited for the line of cars to move.

'That's good.'

Philippe and his family had looked nice. They weren't our usual type of mark. My new-found honesty seemed indeed to have triggered my once dormant conscience, because all of a sudden it bothered me that we planned to steal a few pounds from people who could so obviously afford it. It had never worried me before.

'I gave Father O'Mara my mobile number. He was keen on getting us to sign up as helpers for the autumn bazaar.'

'Naturally you made sure Philippe was in earshot to get your digits?' I didn't know why I was asking; of course Charlie would have made sure he had ample opportunity to get her number.

'I don't have to help with any bazaar, do I?' Kip tore his attention away from the McDonald's menu.

'No, of course not. Unless you want to donate one of your models to raise money for the church roof?' Charlie rolled the car up to the service window and we ordered our takeaways.

We carried on down to the collection point. 'I don't have to, do I?' Kip persisted.

'No. Charlie was joking, weren't you, Charlie?' I glared at my sister. She should know better than to wind Kip up like this. He was already stressed out from the trip to church and having to deal with being around so many people.

She took the bags of food from the guy at the window and dumped them on my lap along with the drinks. 'I was kidding, Kip.'

'I want to show Sophie my models.'

Charlie slammed on the brakes so hard I nearly had Coke and milkshake all over my best suit. 'Who's Sophie?'

The car behind us beeped its horn.

'She lives next door. She has a rabbit,' Kip mumbled through a mouthful of fries.

'Bloody hell.' Charlie slammed the car back into gear and pulled off again.

Kip swallowed. 'You shouldn't swear when you've just been to church.'

We parked on the drive and Charlie's mobile rang before she could ask any more about Sophie. I clambered out of the car clutching the tray of drinks while Charlie answered her call. After a couple of minutes she snapped her phone shut.

'Philippe got my number from Father O'Mara. There's a charity event his mother is organising for the church and he wants me to help. He's going to meet me at the church hall tomorrow night.' She was unable to keep the glee out of her voice and I didn't think it was simply that her plan was coming together that was making her so happy. I'd seen the way she'd kept sneaking glances at Philippe in church.

Kip rolled his eyes at me as our sister unlocked the front door. A folded piece of white paper lay on the mat.

'It's for you, Abbey.' Charlie picked it up and handed it to me.

I couldn't think of anyone who would want to leave me a note, but the mystery was solved when I opened it.

Abbey, Freddie Davis has people out looking for you and your sister. Call me as soon as you get this. Mike.

His number was below. I couldn't believe Mike had actually followed us up here, and found us so quickly.

I passed the paper to Charlie.

'Damn.' Charlie looked at me keenly. 'And I wonder how Mike knew where to find us.'

'You're swearing again.' Kip made slurping noises with his straw.

'What are we going to do?' I tried to ignore Charlie's steely stare.

She screwed the paper into a ball and tossed it into the waste-paper basket. 'He won't find us. It's just Freddie's ego that's taken a slam. Let's face the facts: the amount of money we got was small change to him.'

She might appear unconcerned but the news had made my appetite disappear. I passed my Big Mac and fries over to Kip. 'Do you think I should ring Mike?'

Charlie frowned. 'And say what? If he asks why

Freddie is so interested in us our goose is cooked because thanks to your weirdo affliction you'll tell him the truth.' She flung herself down on the armchair and kicked off her shoes.

'Maybe you should call him, then.' I would have liked to call Mike but Charlie did have a point.

She flounced out of her seat and huffed her way over to the bin to retrieve the paper with Mike's number on it.

'I thought he gave you a card?'

'Yeah, like I was going to keep it! Honestly, Abbey.' She picked up her mobile and jabbed the numbers on the keypad with short, annoyed strokes.

'Hello, is that Mike Flynn? It's Charlotte Gifford.' Her bare foot tapped impatiently on the polished laminate floor while she listened to his response. I strained my ears to try to catch the conversation.

'No, I'm afraid I haven't any idea why he would be so keen to find us. Some men don't take rejection very well.' Charlie raised an eyebrow and glared at me. 'I'm afraid Abbey is out at the moment.'

My heart did an absurd little flip of happiness that he'd asked about me.

'I'll tell her. Bye.' She snapped the phone shut. 'There, happy now?'

'What did he say?' Kip swallowed the last bite of my burger.

'Freddie has his minions searching for us. Our flat was trashed just after we left.'

'Oh.' I wondered how safe we really were in Wilmslow.

'Mike asked after you. He said to tell you he'd see you around. How did he find us here, anyway?' Charlie's foot was still tapping.

'Um, I may have mentioned it to him when I saw him by the van.' I had to get this lying thing fixed . . .

'Fan-bloody-tastic!'

Kip contented himself with a look as he was finishing up my milkshake.

'It's not as if I do it on purpose.'

Charlie flopped back in her seat. 'Anything else you should confess to? At least he didn't have to snog you to worm information out of you.'

I guess the guilty look on my face must have been the giveaway.

'Abbey and a policeman sitting in a tree, K-I-S-S-I-N-G,' Kip sang from his perch on the sofa. Charlie and I turned in unison to glare at him.

'*So* not helping.' I frowned at him, willing him to shut up.

'Maybe we should try the hypnotherapy stuff again.'

Charlie flapped her hand at him. 'Whatever. But we've got to do something or we're going to be in big trouble. You'll be no use to me on this job if you can't act the part.'

'Don't I have a say in this?' I wasn't sure I wanted to go through the regression treatment again. To be honest, the first time had freaked me out and I was more than a bit reluctant to repeat the experience. I didn't know what else I might see or might be revealed.

'I don't think you've much choice, Abbey. You don't want to go to jail, do you?' Kip's eyes were round and earnest behind his glasses.

I guess when he put it like that I didn't have a choice.

After lunch Charlie put on her pink micro-bikini and a ton of coconut oil before heading into the garden with a rug and the Sunday supplement. It was a shame not to make the most of the early September sun and I wouldn't have minded trying for a bit of a tan myself, but it didn't seem as if she was in the mood for company.

'We could try the CD again now if you like?' Kip had taken Claude out of his cage and put him in his hamster ball. It promptly shot off across the floor and disappeared behind the TV stand.

'I'm scared, Kip.' I could hear Claude rustling about near the curtains and the faint sounds of someone further down the street mowing their lawn.

'Of the regression?'

'Yes.' Even if I could have lied, I wouldn't have. Kip and I had always been close – probably because he was nearer to me in age than Charlie.

'We can just concentrate on the lying if you want.'

'But we tried that last time. I can't control the

images that come into my head and it frightens me.' It was a relief to confess my fears.

Claude reappeared and rolled towards me, his whiskers twitching as he neared my feet.

'I can stop it if you get uncomfortable. We'll agree a signal and I'll bring you out of it. I've read lots more stuff on the Net since we tried it the last time.' Kip scooped up Claude and gave me his best pleading look: the one he used when he wanted to watch something scary on TV that Charlie had banned him from seeing.

'What kind of signal?'

He thought for a moment 'Raise your hand if it gets too much.'

I lay down on the couch and Kip drew the curtains while I made myself comfortable.

'Ready?' He popped Claude back in his cage and placed the disc in the computer ready to begin the session.

My heart raced as he pressed the button before resuming his seat on the end of the sofa. The music started and I tried to focus on my breathing as motes of dust danced in the air in front of me in the dim light. The narrator's voice flowed out of the machine and I closed my eyes.

Kip took over when the narrator stopped and I heard his voice as if it was coming from a long way off, instructing me to lie. Then, without any warning, images began to enter my mind.

I wasn't on the floor like before. I was sitting at a dinner table with crayons in my hand. The TV played again in the background and I could smell vinegar on chips, acrid and sharp in my nostrils. My pulse raced and I knew before it happened what was coming.

There was someone there with Mum in the flat – a man – and they were arguing in the bedroom. Charlie had taken Kip out in his pram and I'd been given chips as a treat to keep me quiet. I coloured a picture of a house and a big yellow sun. The bedroom door banged in the flat and the man came into the lounge.

Back in the present my palms felt sweaty and my arms were stuck to my sides. I wanted to signal Kip, to make it stop before the man turned to face me. Before I saw the face I knew I would recognise. I couldn't move and couldn't protest but even as a four-year-old child I knew I didn't like the man.

'Freddie.' My voice sounded hoarse like a creaky door. I forced my hand up and away from where I had dug my nails into the leather of the couch.

The Celtic music stopped and Kip knelt next to me. His breath felt warm on my cheek as I opened my eyes.

'Abbey? Are you okay? Shall I get you a drink? You look really pale.'

I pushed my hair back from my face, my hands

trembling as I tried to take in what I'd seen in the regression.

'Can I have some water, please?'

Kip sprinted off and returned a few seconds later with a glass. 'What happened? You said "Freddie".'

I levered myself up into a sitting position and took the water. Droplets splashed on to my knees as I put it to my lips to take a refreshing drink and my teeth chattered against the edge of the glass.

'Freddie was in our flat. Talking in the bedroom with Mum. They were arguing about money.'

'Are you sure?' Kip sat down next to me and flopped back.

'I'm sure.' I put the glass down.

He squirmed about on the sofa. 'You don't think there's any chance—' He broke off to stare miserably at the floor.

'Any chance that what?'

'That Freddie might be . . . you know.' He took off his glasses and scrubbed at his face with his hands.

'What?'

'That he might be my dad?'

'No!' I couldn't explain it but I was absolutely certain that whatever Freddie's connection was with Mum, he wasn't Kip's father.

An expression of relief crossed his face but I could tell he wasn't a hundred per cent reassured. None of us knew who our father might be. It wasn't something I'd ever given too much thought to. Aunty

Beatrice had always implied that Mum hadn't been certain who had fathered us either. As I said, none of them had responded when social services had appealed for family members to come forward after Mum had vanished.

'It was a business deal. Something that Freddie wanted Mum to do and she wouldn't. Charlie had taken you out but I'd been ill and it was cold so Mum wouldn't send me with you. Freddie bought me some chips and I stayed in the living room doing some colouring.' I tried to remember more but the pictures were fading. The harder I tried to recall the memory the faster it slipped away from me.

'This was new, then?' He pushed his glasses back up on to the bridge of his nose and blinked.

'Yes, it was different from before, but I guess it must be significant somehow or why else would I remember it?' My head ached and I took another sip of water.

'Do you think we should tell Charlie about this?' he asked.

'Tell Charlie about what?' Our sister appeared in the doorway with a glass of fruit juice in her hand and a sarong draped loosely around her hips. The faint scent of coconut oil filled the room.

'We did another session with the CD and Abbey had another flashback.' Kip filled her in on what I'd just told him.

'I don't remember anything.' She frowned at me.

'Well, except that Mum always mollycoddled Abbey because of her asthma.'

'Maybe you should try the CD?' Kip suggested.

Charlie looked as if her juice had soured on her. 'I don't think so. See what you can turn up on the Net.' She vanished back into the kitchen.

I knew that looking back at the past was upsetting Charlie at least as much as me and somehow I got the feeling that she hoped he'd unearth some kind of miracle cure for me. Then all of these uncomfortable feelings could go back into the box where they had been for the last seventeen years.

Monday morning dawned grey and misty: one of those summer days that start off gloomy but turn hot when the sun burns off the cloud cover. Charlie bustled downstairs in her most demure going-to-an-interview outfit and twirled around in the kitchen for our approval.

'You look great.' I really hoped she would get the charity job. Perhaps she would love it so much that she would settle down and forget about scamming Philippe and his family. Then I wouldn't have to psychoanalyse any dogs.

'I'll be back around three.' She grabbed a slice of toast from the pile I'd just finished buttering.

'Three?' What was she planning on doing for the rest of the time? I thought she'd said her interview was at ten.

'I've a few things to do.' She picked up my cup of tea and took a quick slurp. 'Now I'd better run. Don't want to be late.'

'Good luck,' Kip called as the front door closed and she'd gone.

'What are you doing today?' I tipped the rest of my tea down the sink.

'Searching for information on the Net as instructed. Did you want any more of the toast?' He snatched up the plate and settled down to work.

My day stretched in front of me, long and pointless – more pet research and a stake-out at the park at lunch time. Philippe was reputed to walk his dogs there at the same sort of time every day and Charlie thought I should take a peek so I'd have some idea what I was in for. For my part, I hoped Philippe wouldn't spot me lurking in the bushes. After the supermarket incident, and if he connected me with the church, I could end up being branded a stalker.

I loaded the washing machine with towels and left Kip tapping away in front of the keyboard as I set off for the park. The earlier greyness had gone and the sky was blue and clear. A light breeze ruffled the leaves of the trees as I strolled along the path.

How Charlie managed to source most of her information I'll never know. A lot of it she gleaned from celebrity magazines and fan boards. She trawled the financial papers too, researching facts.

The rest was legwork and stake-outs which was why I was hanging around a park in the middle of the day waiting for a man to walk his dogs. I sat down on a bench near the main car park and fished a book on dog care and an apple out of my handbag.

It was peaceful in the sunshine with the birds tweeting. A few office workers were sitting on the grass with their packed lunches. The men had loosened their ties and the girls hitched up their skirts, exposing fake-tanned legs to the late summer sunshine. In contrast I felt pale, pasty and overdressed.

'Is this seat taken?'

Mike appeared from nowhere to sit beside me. Dark glasses shaded his eyes so I couldn't read his expression. The scent of his cologne filled my nostrils, faintly woody, spicy and male. In an open-necked shirt and snug-fitting faded denims he looked like any other guy out for a stroll in the park, except sexier.

'Are you following me?' I pretended to be busy with my book and tried to ignore my racing pulse.

'Maybe.' He stretched his arm along the bench behind my back.

I didn't know if I should be flattered or frightened by his reply. Out of the corner of my eye I spotted Philippe and what looked like two wolves on leashes heading towards us.

'Why are you so interested in me and Charlie?' Hopefully he wouldn't notice me watching Philippe over the top of my book.

Mike lightly ran his fingertip along the bare skin on the top of my arm, making my flesh goosebump in delight. 'I'm more interested in why Freddie Davis is so keen to track you down and where exactly you and your sister fit into my investigations.'

Not the most satisfactory of answers. I couldn't tell if flirting with me was a perk of his job or if he actually fancied me. Philippe unclipped the leads on the wolves and they came loping down the path. I raised my book slightly higher to shield more of my face as Philippe jogged along behind them.

'I don't think we *do* fit into your investigations.'

Please don't let him ask me too many questions about Freddie.

One of the wolves paused by the bench and sniffed at my ankles. Instinctively I leaned closer to Mike. Why did Philippe's dogs have to be Alsatians? Of all the breeds he could have owned he had to possess the one that scared me the most.

'Don't you like dogs?' Mike asked as the wolf padded off after its mate and I relaxed back against the bench.

'Small dogs are okay. I'm studying pet psychology at the moment so I'm hoping to overcome my fears.' I felt rather than saw the quiver of suppressed laughter that shook Mike's frame at this little gem.

'Interesting career choice. What about your sister, is she into pets as well?'

Philippe disappeared out of sight with his dogs so

I closed my book. 'My brother is the one that loves animals. My sister has a job interview today, for a secretarial job with a local charity.' I was proud of my answer – telling the truth didn't mean I couldn't be selective. It felt very nice to be nestled up against Mike.

'How very worthy of her.'

I checked his expression but I couldn't tell if he meant it sarcastically. 'How did you find us?'

He moved his arm from my shoulders. 'I have my methods.'

I tucked my dog book inside my bag. It was time I left: spending time alone with Mike was dangerous. I had to remember that. One wrong question from him and I could put Charlie and me in serious trouble.

'Promise me you'll call me if Freddie makes any kind of contact with you.' Mike took off his sunglasses to look deep into my eyes. I tried to read his expression. Concern? Desire – or was that simply wishful thinking on my part? Blood rushed in my ears as he kissed me gently on the lips. Definitely desire.

'What makes you think he'll contact us?'

His mouth was a fraction of an inch from mine and I wanted him to kiss me again. God, I wanted him to keep kissing me.

'Because he's not a man to cross and for some reason he isn't happy with you and Charlie. I can't tell you too much as it's an ongoing investigation but we want him for more than just financial misappropriation.' He stroked my hair tenderly back from my face, exposing the livid mark below my ear. 'What happened to your neck?'

'I was struck by lightning.' Hell, I had to get out of there and fast. My attraction to Mike was making me careless.

'Lightning?'

'I have to get home.' I leapt to my feet.

'Let me give you a ride.' Mike rose to his feet, looking bewildered at the speed of my exit from the bench.

'No, it's fine. It's a lovely day, I can walk.' I suited my words to the deed and hurried off down the path, hoping I wouldn't bump into Philippe and his wolf pack again. All I could do was pray that Mike wouldn't make the connection with the media coverage of my accident and realise I'd been using a false name.

I slowed my pace when I reached the edge of the park. My pulse rate dropped to match and my breathing eased. I wasn't sure if I was scared or reassured that Mike seemed to be keeping an eye on us. On the good side, a desirable and sexy man clearly seemed to find me attractive. On the bad side, the same sexy and desirable man would arrest me in a flash if he learned about the Gifford family's life of crime.

I couldn't be sure what he knew or suspected

about us and our involvement with Freddie. Maybe it was all an act, a way of getting information from me by pretending he was as attracted to me as I was to him. But surely, that buzz of desire, that stomach-flipping leap inside me every time we met, wasn't the result of some chicanery, was it? If it was, then I'd just made a big fool of myself.

My mobile beeped in my handbag to say I'd received a text.

Got the job.

Oh well, at least one of us was respectable and legitimate at the moment, even if Charlie did have an ulterior motive.

'Abbey?'

A sleek black sports car turned the corner and crawled along beside me. Its roof was down and Mike was at the wheel.

'I said I'd walk. They arrest people for kerb-crawling, you know.' Argh, why was he following me? I needed time to get my head together.

'I wouldn't be crawling if you'd get in the car.'

'Go away.'

'I promise I'll behave.'

A blue Mini behind him beeped its horn. This was ridiculous.

'Men!' I stopped and wrenched open the passenger door. Mike waited for me to climb in before pulling off with a smile and a wave to the driver of the Mini.

'Isn't this better?' Mike switched on his CD player and the sound of soft classical music filled the air.

I didn't answer him, instead folding my arms in preparation for the short drive home. The fewer things I said, the less risk there was of my saying something inappropriate.

We drew to a halt outside the new house.

'Thank you for the lift.' I tried to make my voice sound icy and polite but secretly I hoped he would kiss me again before I got out of the car.

'Aren't you going to ask me in?'

He still had his sunglasses on, so I couldn't tell if he was serious or teasing me until the corner of his mouth quirked and then I knew he was winding me up.

'No. I have to go and check on my brother. He's not good with strangers.'

'You seem very close to your brother and sister. You never mention your parents. Are they still alive?' Mike pushed his glasses up over his forehead so I could see his expression. He looked thoughtful, as if this was some puzzle that had been bothering him.

'I don't know. Our mother vanished when we were children. Charlie brought up me and Kip. We don't know about our fathers.' Even as I spoke a cold, all-too-familiar sinking feeling of desolation filled me. We were different from other people. The only certainty in our lives was that we had each other. I braced myself for more questions.

'I'm sorry. That must have been very difficult for you all.' His voice sounded tender and a little of the ice in my stomach thawed.

'It was. It is. We recently found out that Freddie Davis knew our mother. We have a photograph of him and Mum together.' I had no idea why I felt compelled to share this with Mike. No idea at all, except the nagging suspicion that Freddie knew something about my mother's disappearance, and that Mike could help us.

10

The front door of our house opened just as my mobile rang. I dived on my phone while watching to see who was coming out. A slim female figure with blond hair appeared and scuttled across the garden to disappear into the house next door. I didn't need to be a detective to figure out that it had to be Kip's new friend, Sophie.

I pressed the button on my phone and said hello without checking the caller display, since I expected it to be Charlie.

'Abigail?' It was a man's voice – and not one I recognised. He sounded gruff and uneducated.

'Yes?' Apprehension crept into the pit of my stomach and made me feel sick.

The sneery voice continued. 'My boss isn't too happy with you, or your la-di-da sister. Better watch your step, girlie. Accidents are easy to arrange.'

I cut the call off without replying.

'Abbey? Is something wrong?'

I'd forgotten Mike was still sitting next to me. 'It was a man. He threatened me.' The phone slipped through my fingers and Mike grabbed it instantly, presumably looking to see if he could trace a number.

'Did you recognise his voice? What did he say?'

'He said to watch my step and that accidents were easy to arrange.' I couldn't quite believe what I'd just heard. How had anyone managed to get my number anyway?

'Was it Freddie?' Mike handed me back my phone. Clearly the information he'd been seeking wasn't there.

'No. I don't know who it was. He knew my name, though.' My body gave an involuntary shiver. This was creepy.

'Who would have your number?' Mike demanded.

'I don't know. Charlie, Kip, my aunt Beatrice, the doctor ... that's about everyone, really.' Then I remembered Charlie getting the call from Freddie before we left the old flat and tossing her mobile into the drawer.

I knew she'd bought a new one since. She often changed phones or SIM cards once a job was completed. Since only family members had my number, my phone had stayed the same. It would have been unusually careless of Charlie not to have wiped the memory on the phone before leaving it behind, but, thinking back, I reckoned that that was what must have happened.

Mike drummed his fingers against the steering wheel. 'Maybe I should call this in, get you some protection.'

'No!' I opened the car door, my heart banging against my ribs in my panic to get out of the vehicle.

Mike pursued me up the front path. 'Abbey, I'm not sure what it is that you've done, but I don't think you or Charlie understand what you've stumbled into with Freddie.'

'I told you. It's okay.' I scrabbled about in my bag for my keys and in my haste they went flying out of my hand into a big green bush.

Crap.

Mike dived into the bush at the same time I did. He beat me to the keys, emerging with a triumphant smirk and my 'Groovy Chick' fob dangling from his fingertips. I picked bits of twig out of my hair as he proceeded to unlock the front door for me.

Kip must have heard us coming because he was nowhere in sight as I stomped my way into the lounge.

'A cup of tea would be good, thanks.' Mike relaxed back on the leather sofa as if he were welcome.

'You want tea.' I tried glaring at him but he appeared impervious to my displeasure.

'No sugar. Oh, and a biscuit would be nice.'

Ratbag. He knew I wanted him gone.

The front door banged as I faffed around in the kitchen and wondered if I could get away with poisoning Mike's drink.

'Hello, Charlie.'

I heard the hint of laughter in Mike's voice before

Charlie shot into the kitchen and pulled the door closed behind her.

'Why is there a policeman sitting on our settee?'

'Would you believe me if I told you he followed me home?' I pulled the canister with the tea bags from the shelf and plopped the bags in the mugs. 'Oh, wait, yes, you'd have to.'

'And you're making him tea?' Charlie hissed.

'Listen, we've got bigger problems than the fuzz.' I told her about the creepy phone call.

'Damn.' She opened the kitchen door a crack and we peeped through to see Mike still sitting on the sofa checking messages on his mobile. It didn't look as if he planned to leave any time soon.

'Now what?'

'We need to get rid of him. Leave this to me.' Charlie picked up the tea and sashayed through to the lounge.

Since she'd stolen my mug, I picked up a packet of custard creams and followed after her to watch the fun. Even so, jealousy gnawed at my insides as my sister settled herself down next to Mike and handed him his drink.

'Abbey told me all about that dreadful phone call. It's very kind of you to offer to protect us.'

Jeez, give me strength . . .

'Freddie Davis has been implicated in some extremely serious criminal activities. If the threats Abbey received are from him or from someone in his employ, I'd advise you and your sister to take them very seriously.' The humour had gone from Mike's face.

'I can't imagine why he'd want to threaten us.' Charlie pouted over the rim of her mug, her big green eyes fixed on Mike.

He shifted in his seat. 'I checked out you and Abbey on our database and you both show up as clean. At this point in time I just want to nail Freddie Davis so I'm prepared to turn a temporary blind eye to whatever stunt you two may have been up to.' He met Charlie's gaze head on and my lungs tightened in fear.

All credit to my sister, she never even blinked. My face, however, felt as if it was on fire and I needed to grab my inhaler from my bag.

'Freddie Davis is a no-good lying scumbag. He was also connected somehow to our mother. Did Abbey tell you about her disappearance?' Charlie pulled the box we'd brought from Aunty Beatrice's from the side of the sofa and waved the picture of Mum and Freddie under Mike's nose.

I could hear myself starting to wheeze.

'Yes, she mentioned that. If I check out what I can will you girls promise to let me know if you have any other calls or incidents?' Mike asked as he studied the picture.

I nodded as I took a puff from my inhaler. 'Of course,' Charlie agreed simultaneously.

He finished his tea. 'Make sure you do.'

Charlie smiled sweetly. 'We promised, didn't we?'

Mike stood up and tucked the photograph into the back pocket of his jeans. 'I'd better get going. I'll be in touch with you soon.' He directed the last statement at me as I recovered my breath and my wits.

'Bye.' Damn, my voice sounded as husky as Charlie's as he saw himself out of the house.

Kip appeared at the top of the stairs as soon as Mike had gone. 'Why was the policeman here? Are you in trouble, Charlie?' He sidled down the steps with an anxious expression on his face.

'No, we're not in trouble.' Charlie reached out and hugged him as soon as he drew near her. 'Mike's going to help us try to find out more about Freddie's links to Mum.'

'Are you sure?' He extricated himself from Charlie's arms and looked at me for reassurance.

'Yes. He's taken the photo of Freddie with Mum and he's going to look on the police computer.' At least Kip would have to believe me, since he knew I couldn't lie. Maybe there was a positive side to my accident after all. I had suddenly become trust-worthy.

The rest of the week passed quite quickly. Charlie went out with Philippe to help at his mother's 'repair the roof' fundraiser at the church. They were chaperoned by his kid sister, Maria, and half the women's Bible study group, so I think Charlie's style was a little cramped. Even so, she arrived back home all flushed and giggly so I assumed it had gone well.

I was kept busy observing Philippe's dogs at the park and reading up on animal behaviour. The more I saw of them the more worried I became about my ability to convince anyone that I knew anything at all about animal training and psychology. I was fine when it came to the theory but in reality I broke out in a cold sweat whenever I saw them.

Kip continued trying to help me relearn how to lie and researching the nightclub party that was mentioned on Mum's invitation. He uncovered all sorts of information. Most interesting to us was the mention in the press of the celebrities who had attended the opening. It became even more interesting when he managed to get a list of the managing directors of the company that owned the building. Guess who was listed as owner and director?

Fat Freddie.

At least there were no more scary messages. Mike texted me twice. Little caring messages. *U ok? No more probs?* And *Look forward to C U soon.*

In some ways, it would have been nicer if he'd called. There's something about his voice that sends my middle to mush but it's not so good if he asks me questions. With text messaging I could lie – not that

I needed to, as I hadn't anything to lie about. Well, not unless he asked me any probing questions about why Freddie was after us.

Charlie had been given the go-ahead to start her new job with the charity on the following Monday. She'd kitted herself out with two nice new business suits from Next and secured a lift from Philippe to help with the under-tens' sports party on Saturday night at the church hall. I had to admit it gave me a frisson of secret glee to imagine my immaculate sister marshalling a mob of football-mad ten-year-old boys.

When Saturday evening arrived Charlie jumped into Philippe's sports car and headed off for the church hall. I settled down on the sofa with Kip for a night of crap TV and take-out pizza. Charlie might be stuck at a crummy church hall with a bunch of pre-adolescents but at least she had a date. My Saturday night looked less appealing by the minute as I checked the TV magazine.

'Do you want the piece with the mushrooms on it?' Kip's hand hovered over the open pizza box.

I shook my head and he dived in.

'Do you want the last of the Pepsi?' He wiped sauce from the corners of his mouth with the back of his hand.

'Nope, knock yourself out.' This was going to be a long night. It looked as if the highlight of the proceedings would be watching Miss Marple at nine on the cable channel.

I flicked between shows as Kip downed the last of the pop straight from the bottle. He set the empty container back on the table with a loud burp.

Gee, my life was fun . . .

The doorbell rang and Kip jumped up like a shot. 'Erm, that'll be . . . Erm, er, that'll be for me.' He hurtled into the hall, pulling the lounge door shut behind him. I had to crane my neck and peer out of the front window to try to see who was at the door. He had clearly been expecting someone to call.

Kip never had callers. Whenever the door bell went he usually hid in the bathroom or under his bed. He never spoke to anyone except me and Charlie unless he absolutely had to. Sophie. It had to be Sophie – the mystery girl from the house next door. I came away from the window and strained my ears trying to decipher the murmured conversation in the hallway. The door reopened unexpectedly, bumping against my ear.

'I'll be back later. Sophie's cat's had five kittens. Bye.'

Before I had a chance to react the door had closed and he'd gone. My curiosity over his new friend was killing me. I tripped over Aunty Beatrice's box in my rush to get back to the window to try to get a glimpse of our mystery neighbour. All I got for my trouble was a bruised shin and a fleeting glimpse of blond hair.

Great. Now it was just me on my own with no

Pepsi, some pizza crumbs and Miss Marple. There seemed little point in sitting around like a saddo watching an old lady play detective so I decided I might as well go for the full girly night in. Twenty minutes later I was armed with a block of Cadbury's finest and back on the sofa, dressing gown on, face pack in place, and a bumper bottle of WKD Blue at my side.

I'd just got comfy filing my nails and singing along with the music channel's top one hundred songs to play at your wedding when the doorbell went again, right in the middle of Robbie Williams.

'Why didn't you take a key?' I opened the door without thinking, expecting to find Kip standing there. Instead, my own personal policeman was on the doorstep.

Mike grinned at me. 'I thought someone was strangling a cat in here.'

At least he couldn't see how red my face had gone under its coating of green mud.

Crap, the face pack.

'What do you want?' Okay, not the most gracious of welcomes but he could have called first to check if I was in and to let me know he was on his way. It was Saturday night after all, and I might have had plans.

He produced a bottle of wine from behind his back. 'I brought a drink and some information about the photograph.'

'You'd better come in then.' I let him into the

lounge and excused myself to run upstairs. Free of my mud pack, I spritzed on some perfume and hid my fuzzy bunny slippers in the bathroom. I toyed with the idea of getting changed but I didn't want him to think I'd put myself to any trouble just because he'd turned up.

It wouldn't be so bad if he didn't always look so bloody yummy every time I saw him. I don't know what make of aftershave it was that he usually wore but the makers must put some secret pheromone ingredients in it. How else could I explain the effect it had on me?

By the time I'd sprinted back downstairs – slowing my steps in the hall, of course, so he wouldn't think I was eager – Mike had made himself at home on the sofa and was munching on a chunk of my Dairy Milk. I took a seat next to him and moved my WKD before he could snaffle that too.

'How do they get in and out of those outfits anyway?' he asked as we watched an American girl group shake their stuff on the music channel, which had finished the wedding songs and was now on to the top fifty hottest videos.

'You said you'd found out some information about my mum and the photo with Freddie?' I took control of the remote and turned off the TV.

Mike raised an eyebrow and dug into the back pocket of his jeans to produce a small notebook. His leg felt warm against my thigh. 'Yes. I did some digging around, read back through the original investigation reports and found out a few things.'

'And?' All of a sudden I felt shaky and I wished the others were here.

Mike leaned forward and flipped open his notebook. 'The photograph you gave me was probably taken at the wedding of Jimmy "Teflon" Dykes. He was a well-known fence. He and Freddie were very pally around that time and they had attracted some interest back then from the fraud squad. Your mum knew a lot of people who were associates of Teflon and Freddie. By the time she disappeared a few years later it seems she was dating Teflon's brother.'

I assumed that Teflon had got his nickname from not having any charges stick to him. After all, I watch TV, I know about this kind of stuff even if it did sound quite surreal now that it was actually happening to me. It was more like an episode of *The Bill* than real life.

'Okay.' I wasn't sure where this potted history was heading.

'After your mum disappeared, Freddie and Teflon stopped associating with one another. Teflon's brother Harry – your mum's boyfriend – vanished too. I've talked to a few people and it seems there was a big row about some kind of dodgy big money deal between Freddie and Teflon. At the time it was thought that Harry had gone abroad with some of the cash, but now it seems no one has seen or heard from him since the time your mum disappeared.'

I was confused. 'You think he and Mum went off together?'

Mike closed the notepad and rested it on the arm of the settee. His face was earnest as he spoke. 'Abbey, there's no easy way to say this, but I think it's more likely that your mum and Harry are both dead. Neither of them has been seen, their bank accounts remain untouched and no one has heard anything from either of them in all this time.'

Even though I knew, deep in my heart, that my mum had to be dead, I still didn't want to hear Mike say it out loud. For some crazy reason I'd thought this conversation was leading up to her being in hiding on the Costa Del Sol or something. How stupid was that?

'Abbey?' Mike took my hands in his. I wasn't capable of speaking for a minute. Even though common sense told me that he was simply confirming what I'd always suspected, until Mum was found I'd always have that little bit of hope inside me.

'It's okay. I don't know why it came as a surprise. I – we – have always thought she was probably dead.' Now my tongue was functioning again it felt nice to have Mike hold my hands. I couldn't tell him about my secret hope that somehow Mum might still be alive. He'd think I was an idiot. 'Are you allowed to be telling me all this? Doesn't it break some secret police code of ethics or something?'

'No, not if I believe that the information might help secure the arrest and conviction of a fraudster and murderer.'

A horrid sensation, like iced water, trickled down my spine and I gave an involuntary shiver. 'Murderer?' my voice squeaked.

Mike's breath blew softly against my skin as he sighed. 'You and your sister picked the wrong man to run up against. I need to find out more about what went on between Freddie and Teflon.'

All the hairs on my arms were standing up in little goosebumps under the flimsy cotton of my dressing gown. 'Can't you talk to this Teflon?'

The corners of Mike's mouth lifted upwards in a faint smile that failed to reach his eyes. 'He died, shortly after his brother and your mum vanished. He was hit by a car travelling at speed as he crossed the road outside a nightclub. The driver was never traced.'

The alcohol and chocolate in my stomach danced around in a sick-making tango as the full implications of what Mike had said became clear.

'Freddie bumped him off.'

11

I'd blurted out my thoughts without thinking. 'Freddie killed him, is that what you meant about him being dangerous?' Did that mean Freddie might have murdered my mother?

'We're not sure quite what Freddie might be capable of. Oh, by the way, I brought your photograph back. I've taken a copy. I hope that's okay.' Mike sidestepped the subject as he dropped the picture of Mum and Freddie on to the table next to the empty pizza box.

'Fine. Thanks.' I couldn't take my eyes off Mum's face smiling back at me from that innocent snapshot. My mind was still reeling from the enormity of what Mike had implied about Freddie's capabilities. Mike had to be mistaken. Freddie was a fraudster, an extortionist – murder was something else entirely.

Wasn't it? Deep inside I knew Mike was telling the truth. Of course Freddie was capable of murder. How had we become involved with him? How had my mother become involved with him? God, what had we got ourselves mixed up in?

'Abbey, is there anything else I should know about that might be connected to your mother's disappearance?'

The nightclub invitation was next to the computer screen with the notes Kip had made from his Net research. I handed them over to Mike. 'We think this may have been where she was going the night she disappeared.'

The crease across his brow deepened as he looked at the card and then at Kip's notes. 'I don't remember reading anything about this in the original investigation reports. Interesting information on the directors of the nightclub.'

I explained about the treasure tin and Aunty Beatrice.

'It looks as if your brother has done a good job following up the clues. I'm impressed.' Kip had tracked down all the press reports and news photographs of the nightclub opening Mum was supposed to have attended. There had been quite a few of the celebrities of the day in attendance and he'd painstakingly followed up as many leads as he could.

'Do you think what we've found might help?'

Mike tore Kip's notes from the pad and tucked them into his back pocket along with his notebook. 'I hope so. This is a good start and I'll do my best to find out something more for you.'

There was a big lump in my throat and I had to

swallow hard a few times to make it go away. 'All these years we've wanted to know what happened.'

He stroked my cheek with the pad of his thumb, wiping away the betraying trickle of moisture. 'I'll do everything I can but I can't promise I'll find a definite answer. It's been seventeen years.'

'I know.' Yet I felt confident that if anyone could get to the bottom of what had happened to my mother, Mike would. Despite the fact that I hardly knew him, I felt safe with him, as if he somehow belonged in my world. There was something solid about him. Something reliable.

Something dangerous. His lips closed on mine and desire shivered through my body, banishing all thoughts of Freddie and my past.

'I didn't think policemen were supposed to get close to people who are involved in their cases.'

Mike traced a line down my neck and into my cleavage. 'Only if they're suspects. You aren't a suspect, are you, Abbey?' His tone was teasing but it was a good job his mouth claimed mine again before I could pant out something incriminating.

I lost track of time as we cuddled and smooched on the sofa. Car headlights outside the house lit up the lounge walls just as things were getting interesting. The sound of the front door opening had me struggling back into a sitting position and tugging my dressing gown back into place. Mike remained next to me with his arm still draped round my shoulder as Charlie came into the lounge, closely followed by Philippe.

Charlie scowled when she saw Mike. 'We're not interrupting, are we?'

I suspected she hoped she *had* interrupted something. Her reaction would have been the same no matter who I'd been with, but Mike's being a police officer simply made the situation worse. Getting close to someone outside the family was risky unless it was necessary to pull off a scam. There were too many possibilities of being caught out in a lie. My new-found honesty made me an especially big risk.

Philippe's forehead puckered as he looked at me, and I knew he'd just made the connection with the doofus who'd stomped on his foot in the supermarket.

'Philippe, this is my sister, Abbey, and her *friend* Mike.' Charlie wiggled her eyebrows warningly at me.

'It's nice to meet you.' I gave my dressing gown another tweak to pull the edges closer together. It was a good job I'd already washed off my face pack.

'You, also. I think we have met before?' He offered me his hand.

I shook it rather carefully. I'd already attacked his foot and didn't want to injure his hand too. I wasn't sure what position he played in. For all I knew he could be a goalie and his hands could be his fortune.

'Yes, we have. At the supermarket.' I could feel

the vibes emanating from my sister's direction and I knew I would be in for a roasting later for not mentioning the toe-treading incident.

'I think I see you at the park often, too.' Philippe shook hands with Mike and took a seat on the armchair.

'I often go there at lunch times.' Crapola! I'd been sure he hadn't noticed me tucked away on my bench behind my book. What had happened to my chameleon-like ability to blend, invisible, into any background?

'Always, you are reading,' Phillipe added.

'She's studying pet psychology.' Mike sprawled back on the sofa, stretching his long legs out in front of him.

'Really? That is so interesting. I have dogs.'

Um, yes, I had noticed the dogs. I smiled politely.

Charlie huffed off towards the kitchen. 'Abbey, can you give me a hand?' she called in her wake.

I wriggled off the settee and followed her, leaving Mike and Philippe to discuss dog behaviour.

'Have – you – lost – your – ever – loving – mind?' Charlie hissed as soon as the door closed behind me. 'What are you doing? And what's this about you and Philippe and a supermarket?'

I whispered my explanation as quickly as I could while she crashed around the cupboards hunting for cups and the cafetière to make posh coffee. Mugs and biscuits from the packet weren't good enough for Philippe.

'I can't believe you were so clumsy. He's a striker with a top football team, recovering from injury.'

'I didn't tread on him on purpose.' I was a bit more concerned that he'd noticed me at the park.

'Then I come back home to find you canoodling with the fuzz.' She carried on chuntering.

There was no answer to that one. I was entitled to canoodle with anyone I liked but I knew it would do no good to argue with Charlie when she was in one of her moods.

'Although, mmm, maybe this could work to our advantage . . .' she muttered suddenly, snatching the sugar from my hand and pouring some into a china dish.

'I'm not with you.'

'Think about it, Abbey.' Charlie clinked teaspoons on to the saucers. 'You dating a copper increases our appearance of honesty and respectability. If we can pull this job off we'll be well out of the frame as suspects!'

'That won't happen if they finger your old mate fat Freddie. He won't go down on his own. Had you thought about that?' I'd been giving it a lot of thought since my recent conversation with Mike and none of the conclusions I'd drawn were proving pleasant.

'No one is going to take any notice of him ranting

on about us taking him for thirty grand. He's going to be too busy trying to save his own lardy arse from doing time,' Charlie reasoned as she balanced the loaded tray in her hands.

As I opened the door for her to carry the drinks into the lounge I hoped she was right.

Philippe and Mike had moved on to a discussion about football. Philippe had rearranged the junk on the coffee table to demonstrate some sort of game plan. Charlie broke up the conversation by moving the pizza box goalposts to put the tray down and Mike ate the chocolate goalkeeper.

'You are liking dog training, Abigail?' Philippe accepted a cup and saucer from Charlie and fixed his gaze on me.

'She's really keen to learn about pet psychology,' Charlie answered before I could open my big mouth and deny that I liked dogs.

I felt, rather than heard, the stifled snort of derision that came from Mike.

'I would very much like to find someone to walk my dogs. My training sessions are stepping up again now I am cleared of my injury and my pets need much exercise and discipline.' Phillipe looked at me.

'Oh, Abbey would love to help out! It would give her an opportunity to practise some of her theory work.'

There are times when I hate my sister. Mike

looked as if he were biting the inside of his cheek in an effort not to laugh.

'Maybe Monday we could meet at the park and you can get to know Rafe and Leon. They are very friendly but . . . what is the word? Lively. My mother is not strong enough to hold on to them and they need much walking. Mama is not really a lover of my pets.' Philippe's cup wobbled on its saucer as he waved his free hand around in his enthusiasm to explain.

'Perfect. She'll do it. I start my new job with the charity on Monday so it'll fit in really well.' Charlie beamed as she offered Philippe a biscuit from a china plate. He waved it away, murmuring something about watching his carbohydrates.

I felt sick.

Mike pounced on the plate. 'You'll look forward to that then, Abbey,' he remarked as he popped a custard cream into his mouth. The laughter in his eyes told me that he knew exactly how I felt about walking Phillipe's wolves.

We carried on chatting about dogs and other animals. It was a shame Kip was missing: he might have enjoyed the conversation. Mike said he had to go as soon as he'd finished his coffee. I felt a bit disappointed as it wasn't all that late but then again he had made the effort to come and spend time with me on a Saturday night. From what he'd let slip while we'd been chatting I'd gathered his free time was at a premium while he was working on a case.

'I'll see you out.' I walked with him to the front door, leaving Charlie to entertain Philippe.

'You and your sister mix in some extraordinary circles. From major league underworld to Premier League football.' Mike halted on the step.

'Charlie knows a lot of people.' I couldn't bring myself to meet his eyes. Guilt prickled at me when I thought about my sister's real motives for dating Philippe.

'I'll see what else I can find out about the nightclub party. In the meantime, promise me you'll be careful, Abbey. Don't underestimate Freddie.' He placed his hand under my chin and gently tilted my face upwards until our eyes met.

My heart bumped against my ribs in an intoxicating mix of desire and fear. 'Hey, I'm going to be walking two wolves on leashes, remember. No one would dare mess with me.'

He silenced me with a long and very satisfactory kiss. 'It's the wolves in sheep's clothing you need to watch out for.' He gave me one last kiss on the lips and strolled down the path to his car. 'I'll call you.'

I closed the door as he pulled away, my pulse still racing and my skin tingling. Charlie and Philippe jumped apart pretty smartly when I went back into the lounge. My sister's face looked quite flushed. My guess was that she was developing more than a professional interest in her hunky footballer.

'I think it is time I went also. My family worries if I am late home.' Philippe got to his feet.

There was something very sweet about him. He wasn't like any other professional footballer I'd ever read about. The glamorous lifestyle didn't seem to have affected him. He had a kind of old-world courtesy about him and he and my sister looked good together. This time it was my turn to sit on the sofa and wait while Charlie saw off her beau. It seemed to take her quite a while before I heard the silky hum of Philippe's expensive motor pulling away.

'Right, tell me everything.' Charlie marched back into the lounge, the dreamy expression in her eyes evaporating swiftly as the interrogation began.

I told her what Mike had told me about his investigations into our mother's disappearance. It didn't feel any more real as I repeated the information that I'd been given.

'Murder? Freddie, a murderer?' The combative glint in her eye disappeared and she sank down next to me on the sofa. 'Does Kip know anything about this? He'll get really wound up if he finds out.'

'Kip wasn't here. He's gone out. Hadn't you noticed?'

'Out? I thought he was in his room.' She looked at me as if I'd grown an extra head.

'Nope, he's next door with the mysterious Sophie.

Apparently her cat's had kittens.' Personally, I thought it was fantastic that Kip had made a friend. I knew Charlie had spent hours worrying about Kip and what the future might hold for him, as I had myself. It was why we'd come up with the plan for the farm.

Charlie slumped forward and put her head in her hands.

'Char . . . you know, we could just forget about this latest job. I mean, Kip seems happy and this house is nice . . .' I ground to a halt. If Kip could start to settle and make some friends, lead a more normal life, then we could give up our life of crime. Charlie and I both wanted the same things for him; if I could persuade her to drop her crazy scam perhaps we could make a new life here in Cheshire.

We could have a new dream, one for me and Charlie. A nice little house and normal jobs. We could make friends, settle down and live the way other people did. We wouldn't be the odd ones out any more. I knew that Charlie hankered after that kind of normality the same way Kip and I did.

She lifted her head and leaned back against the sofa with her eyes closed. 'We can't. We need the money – lots of money. The charity job won't pay enough to cover all of our rent for this house and even with Kip's benefit allowances we wouldn't make enough to keep us going. The valuables that Bella keeps in the safe at Philippe's house would set us up for the farm. We'd have a proper home, Abbey. Kip would feel safe and we could finally have a normal life.'

'But Philippe seems so nice. You genuinely like him, don't you, Charlie? How can you rob him?' I'd been puzzling over this. He didn't appear to fit our usual criteria for a mark. Charlie wasn't hard-hearted but I had started to wonder if she was becoming addicted to the buzz of pulling off a successful scam.

'I do like him. I *really* like him. But the money and jewels in his safe aren't personal things. They're well insured and besides, a lot of it came from Philippe's grandfather and he was not a nice man. Trust me, Abbey, most of the goods Bella has hoarded away weren't come by honestly.' She opened her eyes and blinked.

'But they go to church and do charity work and everything. It doesn't make sense.' I was struggling to take in what Charlie was saying.

'Guilt. Good old Catholic guilt. Besides, it wasn't Bella who stole the money or the jewels. Philippe told me she only keeps them because she promised his grandfather on his deathbed that she would never dispose of them. She's all about family. We'd be doing her a favour, really.'

'Mmm.' Somehow I wasn't convinced and I suspected Charlie was attempting to dispel her own hidden doubts. It looked as if I was still down for the dog patrol, though. I would have to try harder to change her mind.

Something yellow flitted past the lounge window and there was a rapping on the front door.

'Looks like Kip's come home.' I got up to let him in and he burst through the door.

'Thanks, Abbey. Is Charlie back? Sophie says I can have a kitten in a few weeks when it's old enough to leave its mother. They're so cute.'

I could see Charlie shaking her head behind his back through the open lounge door. 'Um, that's nice, but I'm not sure Claude would be very happy if you got a cat.'

He kicked his trainers off in the doorway and hurried through into the lounge to appeal directly to Charlie.

'I could keep them apart and they would soon get used to one another.' He flung himself on to the sofa next to her and picked up the last of my chocolate from the floor where Charlie had moved it when she'd set the coffee tray down.

'When we buy the farm then you can have a kitten.' Charlie looked hard at me.

Kip's face fell. 'That could take ages and Sophie will need to find homes for them all before then.'

I could feel an argument brewing. Kip had clearly set his heart on getting one of Sophie's kittens. 'They won't be ready for quite a while yet and you can see them every day,' I suggested. 'Perhaps nearer the time when they can leave their mum we'll see if you can have one.' It usually fell on me to act as peacemaker between Kip and Charlie.

'When do we get to meet Sophie, anyway?' Charlie asked.

Good question. All I knew about her was that she was small and slim with blond hair, lived next door, and had a rabbit.

Kip frowned. 'She's our neighbour. You can say hello to her any time. She's really nice.'

'How old is she?' I'd got the impression from the glimpse I'd had that she was about Kip's age.

'I don't know, my age I think. She starts college soon, though.' Kip looked vague and I knew Charlie and I wouldn't get much more information out of him. 'Was Mike here earlier? I thought I saw his car.'

Charlie flashed me a warning glance.

'Yes. He brought back the photo of Mum and Freddie. I hope you don't mind but I gave him the notes you'd made about the nightclub invitation.'

'That's okay. I've got copies. What had he found out?'

Charlie rushed to give him a carefully edited version of what I'd told her before my honesty bug could kick in and spill the beans. Neither of us wanted to scare him with an overload of information. He has a very active imagination and he takes virtually everything he's told literally. Mike's info had frightened me and if Charlie were to be truthful I think she'd say it had rattled her confidence too.

'So this Harry bloke disappeared as well? Wow, maybe I should see what I can find out about him.' He sounded excited at the prospect of something fresh to research.

It would be hopeless for me or Charlie to try to stop him. He loves to look things up and we knew he would be trawling the Net for information at the first available opportunity. I just hoped he wouldn't uncover anything too unsavoury. Whilst his hacking skills were quite useful to us, it was a double-edged sword while there were sites out there that we didn't want him to find.

I wondered if Mike would turn up anything new on the nightclub party. I wasn't certain where I stood with him. It was a bit weird. I mean, I knew he liked me and everything, but were we dating? Were we a couple? I didn't know anything much more about him than his name, mobile number and job. A few cute texts and some kisses didn't make a relationship, did it?

We'd talked a little while we'd been on the sofa but not in any great detail. We'd been too busy doing other, more interesting things. Maybe I needed to get Kip to do a bit of investigating for me while he was busy surfing the Net. It would be nice to know a bit more about the man I couldn't stop kissing.

12

Charlie dragged me off to Mass with her again the next morning. We left Kip at home; his one and only experience of church had been more than enough for him. I had a hunch that he'd be round to see Sophie before we'd even made it to the end of the road. What I hadn't figured out, though, was which was the bigger attraction to Kip – Sophie, or her pets?

Philippe's car followed ours into the car park. I watched through the driver's mirror as he helped his mother from the car then opened the rear door for his little sister. Charlie was busy fussing about and picking invisible bits of lint from her suit. I decided to test out her real feelings about her new man.

'Your Philippe has a nice bum.' I waited for her response.

'He's not *my* Philippe.' She glared at me, a pink tinge in her cheeks.

We left the car and headed towards the church. Charlie strutted along with righteous indignation in her step. My comment about Philippe had clearly hit a nerve. It looked as if my suspicions about how much she liked him were correct.

There was a knot of people at the church door, all busy chatting. Philippe's mother was in the thick of the group, and I noticed her small dark eyes narrow as Charlie and I approached.

'Ah, Charlotte, thank you so much for your assistance yesterday. Philippe has told me how helpful you have been.' Bella's smile didn't reach her eyes despite her soft words. She had the same lilting accent as Philippe but her voice held an underlying edge of steel. I could see why her son didn't seem to be one of those flash-car-driving, heavy-drinking, falling-out-of-nightclubs types of footballer. At least, not while he lived with his mother.

'Not at all, it was a pleasure,' Charlie assured her.

'Mama, this is Abigail, Charlotte's sister. She is the one who is studying animals.' Bella's shark-like gaze shifted over to me at Philippe's introduction.

'Nice to meet you.' I almost bobbed a curtsey and called her ma'am.

'You look very frail to handle two large dogs.'

'I'm stronger than I look.' I don't know why I assured her of my ability to manage Philippe's mutts. I wasn't terribly convinced myself, but it obviously wasn't a lie – I really am much stronger than I look.

Bella looked doubtful but Philippe's little sister Maria smiled at me.

We filed into church and our respective pews. As

always I followed Charlie's lead when it came to the kneeling, sitting, and standing lark. Secretly, I quite liked going to church. Maybe it appealed to that part of me that craved normality and respectability. There was a sense of belonging, of being part of a group, something I hadn't experienced since I'd been a member of the hockey team at school.

Charlie timed our exit so that we were shaking hands with Father O'Mara just as Philippe and his family were leaving. I liked Father O'Mara too; he cracked little jokes and made you feel comfortable. Bella smiled her shark smile at Charlie, her teeth deadly white next to her frosted-pink lipstick.

'My son tells me you begin your job with the charity tomorrow?'

'Yes, I'm looking forward to it.' Charlie sounded very keen.

'I expect I shall see you there. I am frequently in the offices. It is a cause close to my heart.'

I wasn't sure if this was meant to be a reassurance or a warning. Philippe, however, smiled benignly while his mother continued to talk to Charlie, so I tried to be charitable myself about her intentions.

'Your brother is not with you today?' Bella asked.

'No, Kip wasn't feeling well this morning. His health isn't good,' Charlie fibbed.

'It is better that a family attends church together. Family is very important. Philippe and Maria's papa died when Maria was a baby and we have always been very close.' Bella started to walk towards the car park and we all fell into step to accompany her.

'We agree, don't we, Abbey? It's similar for us. Since the loss of our parents when we were young we've become very bonded as a family.'

I nodded my agreement as Bella looked to me for confirmation. I suppose we had more in common with her than I'd realised. Family came first for us, too.

'My son told me there had been a tragedy when you were young. It is good that you have raised your sister and brother.' Bella actually sounded approving, so perhaps there was hope for Charlie after all. 'I am responsible for arranging the flowers in church this week. Perhaps if you are free on Thursday evening you would be so kind as to help me?' Bella's question was more of a command.

'Yes, I'm sure I could.' Charlie sounded a little stunned.

'Six thirty in the vestry.' Bella turned on her spiky heels and swept off towards Philippe's car with Maria.

He mouthed 'I'll call you' to Charlie, then followed his mother and sister.

'Looks like you're in. Bella actually seemed to approve of you.' I opened the car door.

'I think I'm about to get a bigger grilling on Thursday than a piece of cheese on toast,' Charlie said as she slipped into the driver's seat.

I'd have felt more sympathetic if I'd been able to

forget that my dear sister had forced me into walking Philippe's dogs.

In keeping with my new-found religiosity I prayed for torrential rain and hurricanes for Monday lunch time. However, I was either out of luck or out of favour and the day dawned fresh and bright.

Charlie trotted off for her first day of paid employ-ment wearing one of her new suits and clutching a Tupperware box full of salad for her lunch. I so envied her. I would have given anything to be the one in a nice nine-to-five office job. Kip appeared to have stopped sulking about Charlie's refusal to consider a kitten and had resumed work on his model of the London Eye.

'Does Sophie like your models?' I watched as he painstakingly glued a microscopic piece of balsa into place. There had been a faint smell of perfume in the house when we had returned from church the day before and it wasn't one that Charlie or I used.

'She says they're cool.' He poked his tongue out between his lips as he concentrated.

Ha! I was right. She had been to the house while we were out. 'Is she coming round later? It'd be nice to meet her.'

Kip admired his handiwork for a moment before answering me. 'Dunno. She's really shy and she's got to go to the dentist today.'

Okay. I wasn't going to give up that easily. 'Maybe

she'd like to have lunch with us one day this week.' If it was just me and Kip she might agree to come round and I could get to know her.

'Dunno.' Kip adjusted his model.

'Why don't you ask her when you see her?' I wasn't fooled. I knew he would never say anything to Sophie unless I really pushed him into it.

He heaved an exasperated sigh. 'Okay, I'll ask her – happy?'

'Perfectly!'

He threw a cushion at me when I laughed.

I wasn't so cheerful when it got to lunch time and I had to pull on my tracksuit and make my way to the park. My stomach felt as if it were turning back-flips all the way there. I'd tried to persuade Kip to come with me but without any success. Even the lure of meeting the dogs hadn't worked.

The sound of barking reached me before I rounded the last corner. I paused to take some preventative puffs from my inhaler. It wouldn't look good if I keeled over before I even took hold of the leads. How I'd let myself be persuaded into doing this I would never know.

Philippe had tied the dogs to a bench and was limbering up with some stretching exercises, much to the gratification of the office girls who were eating their lunches in the park. Professional footballers have very nice muscle definition – something I hadn't noticed before.

'Abbey, you are come – wonderful!'

The collective faces of the girly audience fell and I heard one mutter, 'Don't know what he sees in her.' There was a general flicking of hair in agreement with the speaker and my face started to heat up. Philippe, to his credit, either didn't hear the comment or was too much of a gentleman to pick up on it.

'As you are not yet used to the dogs or they to you I think it may be good if we do this together.' He finished stretching out his shoulders and gave his arms a shake before moving to untie the leashes.

I stood a good four feet away from the nearest dog and tried hard to remember what the textbooks had said about asserting oneself as the leader of the pack. 'Sounds good.'

'If you take Rafe – he is the smaller one – I will take Leon. I show you the route I go. It's not far, about two to three of your English miles. We will take it slowly.' Philippe smiled at me.

'Okay.' I was incapable of forming a longer sentence. I wanted to go two to three miles all right – but in the opposite direction and as fast as I could run.

What had those damn books said again? Look, act, and sound confident in order to assert your authority as pack leader. Philippe handed me the lead of one of the wolves. It sniffed around my knees and left a trail of drool on my tracksuit leg. I was aware of Philippe and the girly gang watching to see what I would do.

I remembered that page four of the book had said I should get to know the dog, so I held out my hand for Rafe to sniff and ventured a cautious pat on the top of his massive head.

Philippe beamed. 'I can see Charlotte was correct. You are good with animals, like your brother, so very calm.'

Calm? I was paralysed by fright.

Rafe started to pull on his lead, eager for the walk. I held on tight and we set off at a jog along the path. The leather strap cut into my hand with the strain of the dog pulling against it and I gave a firm corrective jerk as my books had instructed to slow the animal's pace a little. It was a good job I'd used my inhaler beforehand, because Philippe's idea of a slow pace turned out to be my idea of a sprint.

We finally reached the edge of the park, where the open space stretched down to the lake, and thankfully Philippe came to a halt. By now I had developed a chronic stitch in my side and wanted to throw up on the grass.

'I usually let them have a run off their leads at this point. Sometimes I let them go earlier, but it has been good for you to get to know them today.' He jogged on the spot, then released the clip on Leon's collar to let the big dog run free.

Rafe jumped up and planted two large paws on my chest. I staggered backwards. His sharp, pointy teeth were very close to my face and I smelt stale dog meat on his breath.

'Sit!'

Rafe ignored me and whined in my ear.

'Sit!' I gave the lead a downward tug as I spoke, just as the books had suggested. Fear added an authoritative edge to my command. Much to my surprise and relief, the dog sat down at my feet.

'Good boy.' I released his clip and he ran off to join his friend.

'You are fantastic, Abbey. Rafe will never listen to my instructions.' Philippe grasped my hands and squeezed my fingers enthusiastically.

'You have to be assertive. Pack leader.' I was still short of breath.

I could hear rustling and strange sounds like twigs snapping coming from the large laurel bushes to the side of us. If there were squirrels in there they were mighty big ones.

'Come, we walk to the lake and you can tell me more about training the dogs.' Philippe set off again at a brisk trot and I puffed along after him. As soon as we moved a scruffily dressed man appeared from the bushes clutching a camera. Without any warning he started to fire off snaps as if there was no tomorrow.

'What's he doing?' I speeded up to jog along at Philippe's elbow.

'Paparazzi. They are a nuisance; like an annoying fly you can brush them away or ignore them.'

Philippe flicked an annoyed glance back at the photographer.

I couldn't believe someone would want to take photographs of Philippe in the park. It wasn't as if he was doing anything newsworthy. 'Why is he here? I mean, you're just taking your dogs out for a walk.'

The animals in question were sniffing around the edge of the water. Further along the shore a flock of Canada geese hissed and cackled their disapproval of the dogs' proximity.

'I don't know. Maybe it is because I am recovered now from my injury and hope to be named to play this Saturday. Maybe it is because I am out with a pretty girl. Maybe it is a slow news week, I do not know.' He smiled at me.

My cheeks grew even redder. It was nice of him to say I was pretty. Apart from the fact that he kept two big dogs, I really liked Philippe. Charlie would be an idiot if she let him go just so she could grab some cash.

Philippe called the dogs away from the geese by throwing them a stick. He set off after his pets at a faster pace while I slowed down a little to allow the cramp in my side to ease. The photographer had disappeared. With any luck the pictures would never see the light of day. I didn't want to be seen red-faced in a dog-drooled tracksuit by all and sundry.

Eventually Philippe rejoined me and together we called the dogs to heel. It took a few attempts to get them back on their leads and I told Philippe some of the things I'd learned from my dog-whispering studies. He appeared impressed. I had charge of Leon, the larger dog, this time as we walked back to Philippe's car.

'Tomorrow I have training and physiotherapy so it will be later when I bring the dogs. Can you be here at four? If it goes well then you can exercise them for me in the week while I am at the football ground.'

We stopped by his car and I instructed the dogs to sit, pushing down on their rears as I made the command. Gratifyingly, it worked. So far, so good. This whole dog-trainer thing hadn't been as bad as I'd first thought. I didn't feel ready to go solo yet, though.

'That sounds okay.' My sides and calves were killing me; I needed to go home and soak in a nice bath. Too many walks with Philippe and I would be the one who needed physio, not him. I didn't think my sister would want to join him on his excursions in my place, especially not in her usual high heels.

'It has been most enjoyable today. It is good to get to know more of Charlotte's family.' He was as polite and nice as always. My conscience gave me another sharp dig at the ethics of scamming such a nice guy and his family. He was plainly besotted with my sister and from what I could see Charlie seemed very keen on him.

I handed him Leon's leash and the dogs jumped

into the back of his car when he opened the hatch. 'It's been nice to get to know you better, too.'

We said our goodbyes and I set off on my walk home. Since every bit of me felt sore I was tempted to ring for a cab. I don't know why I was surprised when Mike's car appeared at my side as soon as I exited the park.

'Care for a ride?'

'Don't you have a job you should be doing?' I retorted, but opened the passenger door and jumped in anyway. I ached too much to refuse the ride and I liked being with Mike.

'I thought I should make sure that your sister's boyfriend's dogs hadn't eaten you for lunch.'

'Very funny.'

'Did your pet psychology theories translate into practice?'

'It went very well, thank you.' I'd survived unbitten. That counted as success in my book.

Mike grinned. I knew he wasn't fooled by my statement.

A few minutes later we were parked outside the house.

'I suppose you'd like a cup of tea?'

Mike leaned across and kissed me on the lips, sending that lovely, heady, feel-good buzz zooming through my body. 'I'm counting on it.' Again, I wondered what I was doing. However, whenever Mike touched me I didn't really care.

Kip was at the computer when we walked in. Usually he would have bolted if he thought someone he didn't know was in the house. I took this as another sign that our move here had been a good idea. He seemed to be becoming much more sociable than when we'd lived in London.

'Mike, this is my brother, Kip.'

Kip peered at him. 'You're the policeman.'

Mike sat down on the sofa. 'Yes. You must be the guy who'd done such a great job with those notes the other day. I was very impressed at how thorough you'd been. It saved me a lot of work.'

Kip looked embarrassed but thrilled at receiving praise from Mike. Ever since he'd dropped out of school at fourteen he'd never had much social inter- action with anyone. The educational welfare officer had arranged for some home tutoring when our doctor had provided medical certificates under pressure from Charlie, but it hadn't lasted long. As soon as Kip had turned fifteen the system had lost interest, and a year later Charlie had rented a flat on the proceeds from our first scam and we'd liberated Kip from Aunty Beatrice's care. We'd had to wait until he was sixteen as legally it would have proved tricky otherwise, but as soon as we'd been able to we'd struck out on our own. The three of us against the world.

I left them to it and went to put the kettle on, checking my reflection in its shiny stainless steel surface. My cheeks were still flushed crimson and my hair looked as if it had been styled by Ronald McDonald. I splashed cool water on my face and shook my ponytail loose, frantically trying to tidy it up with my fingers before I went back into the lounge.

I made three mugs of tea, tucked the biscuits under my arm and pushed open the lounge door. I was just in time to hear Kip say to Mike: 'Charlie and Abbey are okay. It's not like Abbey could fool anyone, anyway. Since her accident with the lightning she can't tell lies any more.'

Uh-oh.

I could feel Mike's eyes burning into me as I put the mugs down on the table.

'This one has no sugar in it.' I swivelled the handle towards Mike. I couldn't bring myself to look at him. Had he taken in what Kip had said?

'Biscuits. Great.' Kip plucked the packet from under my arm, completely oblivious of the bombshell he'd just dropped.

Silence hung in the air, punctuated only by the sound of Kip munching on the Jammy Dodgers.

'You can't tell lies?' Mike murmured in my ear as I took a seat next to him on the settee.

'No.' *Hell.*

'Interesting.' His breath tickled my cheek.

'Not really.' Double crapola on toast.

'We'll see.'

Hell. 'So, why aren't you off interrogating Freddie?' Time to turn the tables or the conversation could get way more interesting than Mike could possibly imagine.

'We have him under observation.' Mike slurped his tea.

'How? He's in London and we're in Wilmslow.' I couldn't figure out why Mike was still hanging around here. I somehow didn't think it was irresistible lust for me that was keeping him up north. He seemed to like me but I couldn't forget that he was on an investigation and one which was closely connected with me and Charlie.

I know it sounds stupid but I'd really started to fall for him in a big way and I just couldn't be certain of his feelings. Maybe I could have been braver and asked him outright but then if he'd asked me the same question – well, I'd look pretty silly, as I couldn't blur the truth. It would be majorly embarrassing if he didn't feel the same way.

'There are leads we need to follow both there and here. I don't just work solo. This is a big operation and as I'm out of my area we have to liaise locally.'

'Oh.' I felt a bit stupid. I'd watched enough cop shows to know by now that they worked in teams. Especially if they needed to solve a serious crime and Mike had dropped enough hints to suggest that they had some pretty big concerns about Freddie's activities. I hoped Charlie and I weren't one of the leads he was following.

'My partner, Diane, is taking care of the team at the London end.'

A shaft of pure jealousy caught me off guard. 'Diane?'

'Yes. We've worked together for the past four months.'

'Oh.' I wanted to ask more questions, like how old was she? Was she pretty? Had he slept with her? The last one took me by surprise as I imagined being in bed and having hot, steamy sex with Mike.

'Are you okay, Abbey? You look a bit flushed,' Kip asked between jammy munches.

'Fine. The tea's hot.' I took a sip to prove the point and tried not to grimace as I scalded the tip of my tongue. Thank heavens he hadn't asked what I was thinking about. As Mike had said, that would be interesting – and embarrassing.

'Chances are I'll be heading back to London before the end of the week.' Mike placed his mug carefully on the coffee table.

'Oh.' Gee, I really was the stunning conversationalist this afternoon. Disappointment squelched over me like a big soggy blanket at the thought of his leaving.

'I had a call from Diane earlier. There've been some developments in the investigation.'

Diane again. Were there developments in the case or did he just want to hop into her bed? This was ridiculous; I had to stop my imagination from running riot.

'Well, that's good, isn't it? I mean – not you

leaving, but that there's something happening in the case.' Maybe I should stick to 'Oh' as a response. Then I'd be less likely to make a fool of myself.

'Will you miss me?' There was a definite twinkle in his dark eyes now.

'Yes.' *Crap again.*

'You really can't tell lies, can you?' he murmured.

I glanced up at Kip but he had turned his attention back to whatever he'd been doing on the computer.

'No, I can't.'

'Really?'

I wished I could. 'Really.'

Mike traced his fingertip lightly along the burn mark on my neck. 'Did your accident have any other side-effects?'

Double hell with hockey sticks. 'I've started to remember things. Things from when I was small, from when Mum disappeared. At least we think they're memories.'

His finger stilled just at the point where my pulse beat. 'I think you should tell me everything, Abbey.'

So I did. I just left out the part about why I wanted to be able to tell lies again. I explained about the regression therapy and Kip showed him the CD. When we'd finished, Mike sat back and raked his hands through his hair.

'Bloody hell.' He shook his head as if to clear his thoughts. He looked at me again. 'Bloody hell.'

Yeah. That about summed up how I felt, too.

'You know that none of what you've told me would be admissible in court?' he said finally.

'I don't think I'd be the best witness in the world. Even I find it hard to believe and I'm the one experiencing it.' At least he hadn't laughed or called me a freak.

'What you've said could prove important.' For once his face was serious. His mobile rang and he pulled it from his pocket to take the call.

'Hi, Diane.' He got up from the sofa with the phone held closely to his ear and moved over to the far side of the room.

He listened intently and kept flicking glances back at me. I tried to overhear the conversation while pretending to tidy the coffee table but I couldn't make anything out. He muttered the word 'okay' a few times and then rang off.

He tucked the phone back in his pocket. 'I have to go back to London straight away.'

'I guess that was an important call, then.' I wondered when I'd see him again, or even *if* I'd see him again. I still wasn't sure how things stood between us. Now he knew my brain had been fried he might not want to see me at all. Maybe he had just got close to me to find out the information he needed. That felt worse than anything.

'It could be. I'm sorry, Abbey, but I can't tell you anything about it.' He sounded as if he meant it.

'I understand.' I might understand but I would still have liked to know what had been said, especially if they were about to arrest Freddie. I went with him to the door.

'I'll ring you as soon as I can.' He looked deep into my eyes and I tried to read his expression. What would I do if he didn't come back? He cupped my face between his hands and kissed me on the lips, making my toes curl with pleasure. Then he was gone.

'I've dropped you in it, haven't I?' Kip asked as soon as I walked back into the lounge. 'Charlie will go mad.'

'It would have happened sooner or later.' I was too tired to worry about it. I was more concerned about this Diane woman and what might have happened in London to make Mike leave in such a hurry.

'So you're not mad?' Kip fidgeted on his chair.

The damage had been done. 'No. I was at first, but not now.'

'Are you going to tell Charlie that Mike knows?'

Crap all over again. We would have to tell Charlie when she got home and she was not going to like it.

'I don't think we have any choice.'

'Sorry, Abbey.'

By the time I'd been and had a bath to relieve the cramping in my calves from my earlier exertions in the park it was time for Charlie to arrive home. I hoped she'd had a good first day at work. It would make telling her the latest happenings a lot easier.

'I am knackered!' Charlie's first words as she let herself into the house didn't bode well.

'Photocopy this, file that, and oh! Charlotte, could you make some more coffee, please?' She plunked down on the armchair and kicked off her heels.

Kip gave me an imploring look. I thought it might be better to wait till after tea before we told her about Mike.

'Bloody stupid job. Bella called in to the office just before I left and gave me a huge list of stuff to get for this flower-arranging effort.' Charlie delved in her bag to produce a sheet of paper. She waved it around. 'Look at this lot. Oasis. What the bloody hell is oasis?'

'Give it to me. I'll go to the florist for you tomorrow,' I soothed her.

Kip brought her a cup of tea and put it by her side.

'I thought all I'd have to do with the flowers was show up at the vestry and stuff some carnations into pots. Thank God Philippe texted me and said you'd done really well with his dogs.' She grimaced and rubbed the arch of her foot, wriggling her toes and stretching. 'I swear I have been up and down that poxy office like a yo-yo. My face aches from being pleasant.'

It sounded like my dream job. I'd love to work in an office. I'd have my own desk with a little plant and a photo frame with a picture of Charlie and Kip in it and I'd happily file paper and make tea all day long. Charlie moaned on until I went to cook tea and Kip escaped to play with Claude.

We finally all sat down with our plates of stir-fry on trays as the evening news was about to begin. I was really only interested in the weather as I still had a forlorn hope that a freak tornado might prevent me from walking Rafe and Leon again tomorrow.

The newsreader dealt with the main news. Then it happened – she put on a serious expression.

'News breaking tonight is that detectives are following new leads in a case that has lain on file for the past seventeen years. The case of the mysterious disappearance of a young London mother, Eulalie Gifford, who walked out of her home leaving three young children alone, has been reopened.'

The picture social services had taken of the three of us as children flashed up on the screen, followed by an excerpt of the original news report.

'Oh my God. Turn the sound up.' Charlie looked ashen as Kip grabbed the remote.

'Shh.' I tried to hear the television.

'Detectives involved in the case have issued the following statement.'

A blond-haired woman with a square jawline and a rather masculine voice appeared above the caption *Detective Sergeant Diane Cope*.

'This particular case has been on file for the last

seventeen years. Whilst we have been working on another investigation a new line of inquiry has recently opened and we will be pursuing this over the course of the next few weeks. We would encourage anyone who may have information relating to the disappearance of Eulalie Gifford to come forward.'

A photograph of Mum appeared briefly on the screen, and then the newscast moved on to the next item. We sat in a stunned half-circle. I don't think any of us could find the right words to express how we were feeling. Shocked, numb, and with a curious sense of unreality as if we couldn't believe that we were on TV, that it was our family they were talking about. After all this time we might get an answer to what had happened to our mother.

Guiltily, I felt a rush of relief that Diane was so obviously not someone Mike would be likely to fancy, even while I panicked over what this new inquiry might mean for us. It sounded as if the information we had given Mike might have provided the police with a breakthrough.

'Well, now we know why Mike had to dash back to London,' Kip finally observed as he shoved a forkful of stir-fry into his mouth.

'You knew something about this?' Charlie speared poor Kip with a steely green gaze.

'Yes. No.' I wasn't helping.

'Make your mind up, Abigail. Which is it?' Charlie turned her wrath on me. I knew she was finding this as painful as the rest of us but being Charlie she channelled her feelings into anger.

Uh-oh. Kip and I did our best to explain. It was a good thing she had no choice but to believe I wasn't lying to her – how perverse was that?

'This is a disaster.' Charlie placed her tray on the floor.

My mobile rang. 'It's Aunty Beatrice,' I said, as I read the caller ID. 'Hello, Aunty. Yes, we just saw the news.' Aunty Beatrice sounded quite perturbed. It must have been a terrible shock for her; at least we had known that there were new leads. I passed the phone to Charlie. Aunty Beatrice still considered Charlie to be the responsible adult and Kip and me merely the children.

We listened as Charlie did her best to reassure our aunt.

'The police are going to see her tomorrow,' Charlie announced as she hung up. 'They want to interview her about Mum.'

'Do you think they've arrested Freddie yet?' Kip asked.

Charlie sighed. 'I don't know. The news didn't mention any arrests.'

'Do you think he'll link us with Mum if they do arrest him? He might blab about the money we took off him.' I really didn't want to go to jail. I'd rather carry on walking Philippe's dogs every day than get locked up.

'I don't know, Abbey. God, this is the perfect end to the perfect day!'

I wondered how Bella would take this development when she put two and two together. Bella was well known for her protective attitude towards her son. I couldn't imagine that Philippe's interest in a girl who was involved in a mysterious crime would go down well with his overprotective mama.

'What have you told Philippe about Mum?' I knew Charlie must have told him something from his mother's comments about the importance of family when we had been leaving church.

'That something awful happened when we were young. We had been left alone and I didn't like to talk about it,' Charlie said gloomily.

That wasn't so bad. 'Philippe is a really nice guy.' I was sure he would understand about Mum and he did seem genuinely enamoured with my sister. When we hadn't been talking about his animals he had been talking about Charlie and how wonderful he thought she was. She wasn't as detached as she pretended to be about him either. It showed in her face every time he called or texted her, and I'd seen her mooning over his photo on the sports pages of the daily paper.

'Yeah, I know.'

'You should call him,' Kip piped up. 'He might have seen the news. Can I finish your stir-fry?' He looked hopefully at Charlie's unfinished tea.

'It's all yours.' Charlie headed for the kitchen to

pour herself a glass of wine from the bottle we kept in the fridge, and to call Philippe.

'Do you think the police will find Mum?' Kip tipped the remains of Charlie's meal on to his plate.

'They might. I suppose something must have happened to tip them off.' I didn't like to think too much about it. Suppose they found her body somewhere? We'd have to have a funeral and everything. The faint hope I'd been nurturing for years of Mum's still being alive was fading with every new twist. I passed my plate across for Kip to finish too. My appetite had completely disappeared.

Charlie was ages in the kitchen. Kip finished eating all the food and announced he was off round Sophie's house. I toyed with the idea of calling Mike. Perhaps he might be able to tell me something or, at the very least, give me some reassurance. Then again, maybe he had just been using me to get information. I hivered and hovered over what to do, and in the end I decided to text.

We saw the news.

I hoped he'd call me back.

Charlie emerged from the kitchen with pink eyes and a half-empty bottle of wine.

'How did it go?' I hoped Philippe hadn't broken up with her. Bella was so protective I could picture her advising him to stay away from our family now we'd become notorious.

She nodded as she resumed her seat next to me.

'He was so nice. All he was concerned about was how I might be feeling. He wanted to come round: he'll be here soon.'

I gave her a hug. Charlie often pretended to be as hard as nails but I knew it was an act. She'd had to become tough and grow up quickly so she could keep us all together as a family. Since she'd been seeing Philippe I'd seen a softer, gentler side to my big sister. She deserved to have someone take care of her for once.

'What about Bella?'

Charlie sniffed and wiped her eyes. 'Philippe spoke to her while we were on the phone. He told her all about Mum and what happened to us. He said she was very shocked but she admires us for coping with everything.'

Even so, I had a feeling that Philippe's mama might well be encouraging him to step back a little from us over the next few weeks. On the bright side, perhaps Charlie would drop the idea of robbing his safe. It didn't seem to me to be the best plan in the world to carry on with the scam if half the media in England were likely to be breathing down our necks. And besides, I liked Philippe.

My phone rang as soon as Charlie had gone up to her room to repair her make-up and change before Philippe arrived. I didn't recognise the caller ID but answered it anyway in the hope that it would be Mike.

'Abigail Gifford?' It was a male voice.

'Who is this?' Suddenly, I was afraid.

'Never mind who I am. Tell your sister she'd better return the cash she stole.'

My throat dried and my tongue felt stuck to the roof of my mouth.

'Who are you?' It wasn't Freddie's voice, but I was sure it was someone he'd employed.

'She's got till Friday.'

The line went dead. Hardened criminals were clearly men of few words.

14

'What are we going to do?' I sat on the end of Charlie's bed and watched her apply her mascara. She didn't seem fazed by the threats. The vulnerability she'd shown downstairs had gone, and she was back to being strong, dependable Charlie again.

'Nothing.' She pushed the mascara brush back in the tube and screwed up the lid. 'There is no way Freddie's getting that money back.'

'But . . .'

She picked up her brush and started to tidy her long black hair. 'Listen, he's just trying to scare us. It's obvious he's in deep trouble and wants to get his hands on some ready cash in a hurry. If we stick it out he'll be under arrest and we'll be in the clear before Friday.'

'I don't know, Char. I'm scared.'

She put down her brush to give my hand a comforting pat. 'I was thinking while I was in the shower. There is no way on earth that Freddie will blab to the cops about us scamming him for the thirty grand. He'd have to answer far too many questions about tax evasion and why he was giving me a big brown envelope stuffed with notes.'

'But supposing he does?'

'Abbey, I'm telling you. He won't.' She put the finishing touches to her appearance and picked up her bag and phone. 'Everything will be fine.'

I wished I were as confident as Charlie. Maybe I should have a glass of wine too: I might become as chilled as her.

She left with Philippe. I watched TV and tried not to think about the phone call. Mike didn't ring. I didn't know if I should try his phone again and tell him about the threatening caller but there didn't seem much point. I couldn't prove it was Freddie's henchman and I didn't want to go into details about the scam (although I was pretty sure he suspected something anyway). Catch-22.

I didn't bother to wait up for Charlie to come home from her date with Philippe. I hoped she was having a good time. Kip had arrived back a little after ten, eaten a huge bowl of cornflakes and gone to bed. He hadn't wanted to chat so I'd followed him upstairs. Not that it did me any good having an early night as I spent most of it dreaming I was being chased by someone demanding money I hadn't got.

Next day, I rolled downstairs feeling crappy with sore eyes and a headache to find that Charlie had already left for work. She'd left me Bella's list of floristry requirements on the breakfast bar with a reminder that I'd promised to pick everything up.

Claude bowled into the kitchen in his exercise ball, closely followed by Kip.

'What are your plans for today?' Somehow I had a feeling they would involve Sophie.

'Nothing much. I'm helping Sophie move some things round at her house and I need to do some more research on the Net.'

It was nice that he'd made a friend. From the way he blushed and mumbled when he talked about her it seemed he'd got quite a crush on our mystery neighbour. Despite our best efforts Charlie and I still hadn't managed to meet her.

I got changed and headed for the florists armed with Bella's list. When I got there it soon became clear that there were too many items for me to carry and the flowers would need collecting on the day. I placed the order and texted Charlie to let her know what I'd arranged.

Next stop was the library to renew the pet psychology books. The place was virtually empty with just a couple of people in the computer suite and an elderly man asleep in the reading room. Mr Biggs, the librarian, took my books and card. One of the daily papers lay open on the counter and I guessed he must have been making the most of the quiet to have a bit of a read.

He noticed me craning my neck to read a titbit of gossip. 'There's a picture in there of a girl who looks like you.'

I froze. 'Pardon?'

'Here, I'll show you.' He flipped a few pages back and there was a shot of me and Philippe in the park. He was holding my hands and it looked as if we were an item.

'It is you, isn't it? With that Colombian footballer.' The librarian sounded impressed.

I read the caption underneath.

'Unknown woman enjoying the company of footballer Philippe Montoya. Her presence seems to be helping the notoriously woman-shy striker recover his fitness following his pre-season injury. Montoya has been named for Saturday's squad.'

There was a whole load more about his team and their position in the league. I skimmed through that part. Thankfully, the article hadn't named me. With Freddie's henchmen on the case, walking Philippe's dogs could bring a whole set of problems I hadn't anticipated. The paparazzi man from the park hadn't wasted any time.

'I'm his dog trainer, not his girlfriend.'

The librarian looked a bit disappointed. I picked up my books from the counter, ready to go.

'I don't suppose you could get me his autograph? It's not for me, it's my lad. He's really into his football.' Mr Biggs stammered a little as he made the request.

Yeah, right, of course it was for his son. 'I'll see what I can do.'

I sent another text to Charlie as soon as I got outside the library to warn her about the newspaper picture. I wondered if Mike had seen it, and just as quickly decided it didn't matter if he had. He knew Philippe was dating Charlie, not me, and anyway, it wasn't as if he was likely to be jealous or anything.

Kip was out when I got home and the house seemed unnaturally quiet. I'm not used to being by myself. Normally Kip was there and since we'd always lived in small city flats I'd constantly had the sense of being surrounded by people. It felt weird to have so much space and solitude.

Philippe had said to meet him at four so I decided to take a nap beforehand. I would need every ounce of energy I possessed if I were to keep up with him and the dogs later. I felt quite decadent as I stretched out on my bed. The curtains were closed, filtering the bright afternoon sunshine into a more muted shade. Outside, the birds twittered in the trees at the end of the garden and I could hear the distant hum of cars passing on the main road. I adjusted the pillows under my head and closed my eyes.

The images were unexpected, flashing into my mind like a movie on the big screen. I was back in the past once again. I was small and lying in a different bed. My eyes were squeezed tight shut and I was pretending to be asleep. I could hear Mum's voice and the sound of laughter. A male voice rumbled and I'd ventured a peep to see what was going on. The door of the bedroom stood ajar and Mum and a man were in the hallway, talking. I couldn't see their faces but Mum sounded excited.

'A few more days and we'll have the money. It'll be a new life.'

She'd glanced in my direction and I'd closed my eyes again quickly as she pulled the door closed.

I snapped awake. My heart banged against my ribcage and my palms were clammy with sweat. My spare inhaler was in the drawer of my bedside cabinet and I took a puff before my lungs could close down in my panic.

What had that meant? Had Mum and Harry been planning to leave us behind after all? Despite everything, we had always clung to the belief that our mother would never have willingly left us. What if we had been wrong all these years?

I tried to control my breathing in order to focus my thoughts more clearly. I wished Kip or Charlie were home. Kip would have come up with a million possibilities for what Mum might have meant and Charlie would have calmed me down by dismissing my fears with her cool logic.

After I'd stumbled to the bathroom and splashed my face with water I tried to rationalise what I'd just remembered. It had to be significant or else why would I have recalled it? I didn't have much time to think about it, though, as it was almost time for me to set off for the park and my dog-walking.

Philippe's car was already in the car park when I arrived. The dogs seemed larger and more boisterous than the day before. I hoped I could remember all the stuff from my studies.

'They are ready for their walk as we are late today,' Philippe announced as he attached the leads and got Rafe and Leon from the back of his car.

No kidding. I had hold of Leon's leash and was almost pulled flat on my face as the dog scrambled for the park. I did my best 'sit and stay' routine while Philippe grappled with Rafe. It took a few goes but I managed to assert my authority. I offered a silent prayer of thanks to my library books.

'Today, I cannot walk so very far. The physio-therapist has told me I must be more careful if I am to be ready for the match on Saturday. I go with you to the field and then you will take the dogs, *si?*'

'Okay.' Crap. Oh well, I guess I had to take them solo at some point and Philippe would be there if I ran into problems. We set off along the path. I kept listening for any suspicious noises in the shrubs. At least there were no hidden photographers this time – well, none that I noticed anyway. I was tugged along at such a pace by the dog that I didn't have much time to check.

Once the dogs were loose I left Philippe resting on a bench and dutifully trotted off after the

Alsatians. I managed to keep them away from the geese and out of the lake. All went well until they spotted something interesting in the undergrowth on the far side of the park and raced off, leaving me panting in their wake.

The edge of the park was fringed by bushes, long grass and trees. I crashed into the shrubs calling the dogs' names. It looked as if I'd stumbled across the area where the local children built their camps as there were traces of fires and flat, cleared spots in the grass between the trees.

Eventually I caught up with the dogs as they sniffed hopefully around a rabbit hole. I wasn't taking any chances of their escaping from me again so I put the leads on before heading back to Philippe.

The dogs greeted him with wagging tails and much joy.

'You are superb with animals, Abbey. Tomorrow, I arrange for you to come to my house and walk them. My mama will be at home and will let you in. Will that be good for you?'

It looked as if Charlie's plan for me to obtain access to Philippe's home was working. My heart sank at the thought; secretly I'd been hoping it wouldn't pan out and we could abandon this scam before it went too far. I agreed to walk the dogs and took a note of his address with a heavy heart. Maybe with everything else that was going on I could persuade Charlie to drop her plans.

Charlie arrived home before Kip, who was un-characteristically quiet over supper and announced he wanted an early night.

'Is he all right?' Charlie asked as Kip vanished up the stairs. 'He didn't ask for more food.'

'He's been out all day with Sophie.'

'Maybe he's just tired then. Or in love,' she suggested.

While Kip was out of the way I told Charlie about the events of the afternoon.

'Guess we take after Mum more than we thought.'

'What do you mean?' I didn't understand.

'It sounds like she was about to pull a scam, too, dummy.'

I hadn't thought of that. I'd always felt that Mum hadn't led a very conventional life. Charlie had memories of us being so poor that she and Mum had lived on noodles for weeks, and times when Mum had come home with loads of gifts for us all. But as for how she got her money, we really weren't sure. What had become clear lately was that she'd mixed in some very strange circles.

'Do you think she planned to leave us behind?' That had been my big fear after experiencing the flashback.

Charlie shook her head. 'No, I think she planned to get some money and take us all off somewhere for a fresh start.' Her tone was emphatic and reassuring.

I felt better when she said that. I could live with

the thought that Mum hadn't been a very moral character either in her choice of men or in how she got her money, but I needed to believe that she'd loved us.

Charlie left me the car the next day so I could get to Philippe's house. She also left me with a list of instructions for casing the joint while I was there. I wondered if he had a pool like the houses in the glossy magazines. Personally, I didn't think there would be much chance to do any snooping under Bella's eagle eye.

Kip's mood was as damp and miserable as the September weather. I wondered if he and Sophie had argued; it could be that Charlie was right and he was lovesick. But I had enough on my plate to worry about without taking on Kip's problems. My own love life looked as if it had fizzled out with a whimper.

There hadn't been anything else on the news about Mum and all I'd had from Mike was a text saying, *b in touch*.

I also had to figure out how to collapse the seats in the new car and secure Philippe's dogs inside it, drive them to the park, exercise them, and get them home again – all under the hypercritical gaze of Philippe's mama. To be on the safe side I'd stashed a supply of dog biscuits in my jacket pockets. I didn't have enough faith in my dog-training manuals to risk not taking a bribe or two with me.

I had been prepared for Philippe's house to be posh but the big wrought-iron gates with security-phone entry system threw me for a loop. On the other side of the gates the driveway swept round to the front of a huge pale pink house built in Spanish hacienda style complete with balconies and potted geraniums. I decided he probably did have a pool.

I parked Charlie's car and pulled the rope on a big black iron bell by the front door. Inside I heard the click-clack of heels on tiles as someone came to answer my ring.

Bella opened the door. 'Abigail, you are come for the dogs?' She eyed my tracksuit and trainers appearance. 'I open the side gate for you. Is better you come round the back.' She waved her hand to the right and closed the door in my face.

I trotted off in the direction she'd indicated, having been duly put in my place. It was obvious she only considered me fit for the tradesmen's entrance. A wooden door opened in the wall and Bella let me into the garden, a lush green paradise. Rafe and Leon bounced across the grass to greet me with joyful barks and Bella wrinkled her nose with distaste.

'Have you got the leads, please?' I almost added 'ma'am' on the end again.

'I fetch them.'

I did my best to get the dogs to sit instead of jumping up and slobbering over me while she was gone. I felt mildly better about being around them but the sight of their big open mouths with their sharp teeth and flappy pink tongues still brought me out in hives.

Bella reappeared with the leashes. It didn't look as if I was going to get inside the house, at least not today. Charlie might come to her senses if I could make her see that this scam was never going to work. I wasn't sure why she was so set on going ahead with it when she and Philippe seemed to be so happy together; all I could assume was that she figured cold hard cash was more reliable than love when it came to securing our future.

'You will take great care of the dogs. My son is very attached to them.'

'Of course.' I slipped the leads on to the collars, doing my best to look like a calm, professional dog-walking kind of person.

'I leave the gate unlocked for your return.' Bella more or less shoved me back out through the wooden door.

The dogs appeared a bit bemused by the small size of Charlie's car but I managed to get them to lie down on the blankets I'd put on the back seat by using some doggie treats to lure them in. Luckily it wasn't too far to the park, and apart from worrying all the way there that they might try to climb over the gearstick to sit in the front, it went better than I'd thought it would.

More bribery got them out of the car once we

arrived at the park and we set off along our regular route. When we reached the open space by the lake I let them off their leashes and took a puff of my inhaler. This was the bit I dreaded. What if they didn't come back when I called them? I hoped they wouldn't take off into the undergrowth again. The earlier rain had stopped but everywhere was wet and I didn't fancy squelching about under the trees trying to flush them out.

My luck must have been in, or perhaps all the church-going had paid off, as the dogs seemed happy just to lope about the field fetching sticks and investigating new smells in the wet grass. I bribed them back with more treats and reattached the leads. We were about to leave when a flash of colour in the trees where the dogs had disappeared yesterday caught my attention.

For a moment I could have sworn I'd seen some-one who resembled Kip: tall, skinny, with auburn hair and a baseball cap, disappearing behind the bushes.

15

I left the dogs with Bella when I got back from the park. She didn't ask me inside the house or offer me a drink. I promised to return the next day to take them out again and went home. It didn't look as if Charlie would be in for an easy ride with the flower arranging. I had the feeling that Bella wanted to see what she could find out about us before we would be permitted nearer the inner sanctums. At present we were still in the same category as the hired help and not on the social circuit of the ladies who lunch.

The doorbell rang as we were finishing supper. Charlie peeped through the lounge window before going to the door. The phone threats had made us more cautious.

'It's Mike, and there's someone else with him. Looks like that woman from the TV.'

Kip collected the trays and disappeared into the kitchen while Charlie went to let Mike in. My heartbeat picked up as I heard the familiar sexy rumble of his voice. If he had Diane with him I assumed it was official business, and whether it was to do with Mum or to do with us, it wasn't going to be good.

Charlie ushered Mike and his female companion into the lounge. Charlie had been right: I recognised Diane as the woman from the TV report. Mike didn't look at me as he took a seat on the armchair and Diane perched on the edge of the sofa. The air in the lounge suddenly felt heavy and oppressive.

'Is your brother at home?' She had a very masculine voice.

'I'll fetch him.' I went to the kitchen to find Kip. My legs shook with every step and my pulse was racing so fast I thought I was about to pass out.

'What's the matter?' Kip's complexion had paled, making the freckles stand out on his face.

'Mike's here. I think it's on official business. They want to speak to all of us together.'

Kip didn't move. 'Are they going to take you and Charlie away?'

'I don't think so. Come on, we have to go and find out what they want.' I grabbed his hand and gave him a tug towards the door.

I half pulled and half dragged him into the lounge. Diane stood up as we entered and we sat down on the sofa next to Charlie.

'This is very formal.' Charlie's voice wobbled.

'There's no easy way to tell you all this.' Mike looked straight at me and I swallowed hard. 'You already know that as a consequence of our investigations into another case we have uncovered new information relating to the disappearance of your mother.'

'Yes.' I grabbed Kip's hand and held it tight. Charlie took hold of me on the other side. We sat united and waited for Mike to continue.

'Earlier this morning we received a tip-off which led us to a woodland site approximately five miles from your mother's last known address.' Diane spoke this time.

'Did you find her?' Charlie barely breathed the question that was in all our minds. Time seemed to hang suspended while we waited for Mike or Diane to answer.

'The remains of two people have been recovered. We are waiting for full confirmation from dental records, but yes, I'm sorry, we think we may well have found your mother.' Mike's voice was gentle and his voice compassionate.

Charlie gasped and Kip choked back a sob. None of us spoke.

'The dental records will confirm your mother's identity but there were certain items of jewellery found at the location which we thought you, Charlie, might remember.' Diane nodded at Mike and he took a small package from his jacket pocket.

I put my arm round Kip's shoulders as Mike carefully unwrapped the folded white paper to reveal the contents. A tiny silvery bracelet, tarnished from its long interment, and a silver brooch shaped like a cat with eyes made from green stones lay on the table before us.

Tears trickled down Charlie's face and she compressed her lips tightly together as she gave a terse nod of recognition. Kip sobbed quietly against my neck.

'What happens now?' I stroked Kip's curly hair.

Charlie pulled a tissue from the box on the table and wiped the tears from her face. 'Will we have to do anything else? Or is this it?'

Diane exchanged a glance with Mike. 'Once the body has been formally identified, the coroner's office will attempt to establish a cause of death. However, until there has been an inquest or someone has been formally charged with your mother's murder, I'm afraid you won't be able to hold a funeral. The final decision will lie with the coroner, but we'd advise you not to make any plans at this point in time.'

'No funeral?' Charlie looked bewildered.

'If formal charges are laid the defence has to agree that the body can then be released. It's to do with ensuring a fair trial. We will, of course, keep you informed if there are any changes in the decision,' Diane explained.

The body. Seventeen years had passed and Mum was now *the body*.

'You may want to consult a solicitor as there

will probably be some media attention, and potentially legal issues over your mother's estate,' Mike added.

I couldn't take it in. 'Does Aunty Beatrice know?' I knew she was a miserable old dragon, but she was Mum's sister and all the family we had left outside ourselves. I doubted that Mum had any kind of estate that would merit a solicitor. It had all been so long ago I couldn't remember what had been decided about the small sums in Mum's accounts.

'Yes, some of our team members are there now. She'll be offered our full support, as will you all,' Diane said.

'I see. Thank you.' Charlie looked shattered.

'Would you like someone to stay with you, answer any questions?' Mike asked. Concern mixed with pity showed in his dark brown eyes as he looked at me and I wished he would take my hand or hug me. Of course that was impossible given his official capacity. But for a moment I thought he meant *he* would stay. None of us answered.

'Victim support will be in touch and they will help and advise you through the next few weeks.' His tone was now clipped and professional, dispelling any illusions I had about his feelings for me. He placed a pile of leaflets on the table. 'We really are very sorry.'

This was it, then. We finally had our answer to what had happened to Mum and I had my answer as to where I stood with Mike. His case was moving on nicely and my assistance was no longer required. He didn't look at me again.

'We're very sorry to be the bearers of such sad news.' Diane sounded sympathetic.

'Thank you.' Charlie stood up.

Mike and Diane followed her lead, both of them looking slightly awkward as if they had expected us to ask more questions. I had a million of them in my head but my thoughts were so jumbled that nothing made much sense.

'Who was the other body?' Kip asked suddenly. 'You said there were two bodies.'

Mike shuffled his feet and I guessed he probably shouldn't have told me as much as he had about Harry and Teflon.

'The identity hasn't been confirmed and the other family have yet to be informed, so I'm afraid we can't tell you any more at this time.' Diane looked uncomfortable and I wondered if she knew about me and Mike. Not that it mattered, as there didn't seem to be a 'me and Mike' any more.

I wasn't certain there ever had been. Everything seemed to be happening together, my life falling apart like a house of playing cards. All I could be certain of was that we were truly orphans now; I was still too numb with shock to process how I felt about my situation with Mike.

Charlie saw them out. Once they'd gone she headed straight for the kitchen, emerging with three glasses and the remainder of the Christmas brandy. She poured us each a generous measure. My teeth chattered against the rim of the glass as I tried to take a sip.

'You're in shock, Abbey. Take a good slug. You too, Kip,' Charlie ordered. I could see she was struggling to stay strong for our benefit, but the news had affected her as deeply as it had us. The taste of the brandy made me shudder as it scalded the back of my mouth and throat. My eyes watered and Kip coughed.

'I'm going to ring Aunty Beatrice.' Charlie knocked her brandy back in a couple of swallows. 'I won't be long.' She disappeared upstairs to her bedroom with her mobile.

Poor Aunty Beatrice. At least we had brandy and each other. She had the police and her memories.

'I don't like brandy.' Kip put his glass back on the table as soon as she'd left the room.

'How are you feeling?' You never knew with Kip, and although we had sort of been expecting this news ever since the day Mum vanished, it had been far more shocking than I had anticipated. Inside I had a hollow, empty feeling now that my hope of ever seeing my mother alive again had finally been extinguished.

'I was scared that the police had come to arrest you and Charlie.' His eyes were pink round the rims where he had been crying. 'They would have taken you away and I'd have had to live with Aunty Beatrice.'

'They won't arrest me and Charlie. Everything is going to be okay. They want to catch Freddie.'

He looked relieved. My inability to lie was good for something.

'Are you upset, Abbey? About Mum?'

I took another absent-minded sip of my brandy and winced as I swallowed. 'I don't know. It's funny, but although I knew something bad must have happened to her and that she was probably dead, I still hoped she'd walk through the door one day.' I finished off my drink. 'Now I know that'll never happen. I suppose I'm just sad, really sad.'

Kip hugged me. I couldn't remember Kip ever hugging me before. Usually all the gestures of affection and sibling reassurance were from me to him, never the other way round.

Charlie came back into the lounge and flung herself down next to me. 'Aunty Beatrice is all right. A uniformed policewoman has been and her next-door neighbour is looking after her.'

'Have you rung Philippe?' She'd been upstairs for quite some time.

'Yes. He was very sympathetic, and suggested I ring Father O'Mara.' She picked up the remnants of Kip's brandy and finished it off.

'That might not be a bad idea. At some point we'll have to plan a funeral and he'll know what to do. I know they said we couldn't do anything yet but it wouldn't hurt to talk to him.'

Kip nodded in agreement. 'Abbey's right.'

I didn't know anything about funerals, or even if there was something we were supposed to do in the meantime. Philippe's suggestion seemed good to me and Father O'Mara was a nice man with twinkly eyes.

'Maybe it wouldn't hurt.' She placed the empty glass back on the table just as her phone rang, the tinny little pop tune sounding startlingly inappropriate.

'Hello? Yes, thank you. It has been something of a shock after all this time.' She raised her eyebrows and mouthed 'Bella' at me before hurrying into the kitchen to take the call from Philippe's mother in private.

'Does Sophie know anything about all this?' I asked Kip.

His cheeks flushed straight away. 'She knows about Mum being missing and all that. She saw the news and guessed it was us.'

'Maybe you should tell her about the police visit before it gets on the TV.'

'Yeah.' Kip stood up and headed for the front door. He seemed pleased to have an excuse to get out of the house for a while. It might do him good to spend time with Sophie.

I poured the last of the brandy into my glass.

'Where's Kip?' Charlie rejoined me on the sofa.

'Sophie's.' I sipped my drink. It tasted mellower than before.

'Bella sends her sympathies. She's taken it upon herself to contact Father O'Mara on our behalf already. She thinks we should have a Mass said for Mum.' She pulled a face. I wondered if she was feeling a bit guilty.

'That was kind of her, I suppose. Did you get out of the flower arranging?' My head felt a bit muzzy.

'No chance. I'm seeing Father O'Mara beforehand and then helping Bella afterwards. She thought it might distract me.' Charlie sighed and eyed the empty brandy bottle. 'How are you?'

'I'm okay.' I took another mouthful of my drink. 'I wonder what she was doing that drove Freddie to kill her?'

'I don't suppose we'll ever really know.'

She was right: we probably would never know for certain. Without any real evidence to link him to Mum's death, we'd probably never be sure that it was Freddie who did it, though by now there was no doubt in my mind. We knew it was something to do with the man she'd been seeing and that a large sum of money was involved – at least, my vision had suggested that. Whatever it was, though, she hadn't deserved to die.

'It's mad, but you know I always hoped she'd come back for us.' Charlie pulled another tissue from the box.

I leaned my head on her shoulder. 'Me too.'

'And now we know it'll never happen.' Her voice cracked.

'It really is just the three of us now.'

We both fell silent at the thought.

After a few minutes Charlie wiped her eyes. 'I thought maybe Mike would have stayed around or phoned to let you know he was on his way back.'

'Nope.' I tried to ignore the hard knot forming in my stomach.

'I'm sorry, Abbey. He seemed nice, too – for a policeman.'

Yeah, well, we were both wrong on that count.

The next morning brought a hangover and an early knock on the door from Philippe's solicitor. The late news had carried the story of the exhumation. There had been floodlit pictures of trees with men in white bio suits looking very busy while the reporter repeated the story of Mum's disappearance with an even graver expression than before. We had decided to carry on as normal. There seemed no point in Charlie's staying home as there was apparently nothing that we could do. I think she would have liked an excuse not to go to work but she wanted to keep on the right side of Bella. It wouldn't have looked good to take time off from a new job even under these circumstances when she wanted to make a good impression.

Philippe's solicitor drafted a statement with us,

which he said he would release to the media. It all felt scarily unreal. He had brought in copies of the morning papers and Mum was front-page news. Grainy pictures of her face stared back at us from beneath the headlines. Inside I still felt numb and empty.

'Are they going to arrest Freddie?' Thankfully, Kip waited till the solicitor had gone before he asked his question.

'I don't know.' I wasn't sure what evidence Mike and Diane might have.

Kip put down his empty cereal bowl. 'But he did it, didn't he? And he wants his money back from you and Charlie.'

'We don't know for certain that it was him, and Charlie says there's no way he can have the thirty grand back.' The net appeared to be closing in on Freddie, though it was still hard to believe that the obnoxious little man with his piggy eyes and fat, pudgy fingers could have been responsible for our mother's death.

'Will we have to move again?' Kip blinked at me.

'I don't know. I hope not. Philippe is very keen on Charlie and I think she's pretty keen on him too. Even if she abandons this scam, I don't think we'll be going anywhere yet.' I didn't want to move. Since we'd come to this house Charlie was working in a regular job, Kip was making friends – it was everything I'd ever dreamed of.

Normality.

'But what if Freddie comes after you?' Kip persisted.

'Then I suppose we'd have to think about it.' I wasn't sure what we'd do. The voice on the phone and the threats we'd received were frightening. It was likely with all the media attention that Freddie would soon find out where we were – if he didn't know already.

It was a relief to get out of the house, even if it was just to walk Philippe's dogs. Bella let me in through the garden door, like last time.

'Your family has made much scandal in the papers.' She thrust the leashes at me, her body oozing disapproval from every pore.

'My mother didn't ask to be murdered and I'm glad she's finally been found. All these years we haven't known what happened to her.' I snatched the leads from her and called the dogs. I didn't feel in the mood to stand and listen to her implied criticism. There had been enough in the press about Mum's lifestyle and none of it had been very nice. It seemed as if Bella disapproved of us after all, despite her kind gestures.

'I am sorry. It must indeed have been dreadful for all of you.' She backtracked a little but didn't sound very sincere. The dogs bounded towards us, excited by the sight of their leads. 'I will see Father O'Mara with your sister tonight. Charlotte tells my son you cannot yet have a burial?'

'No, it's something to do with the legal things.' I wished I could escape.

'I will discuss with your sister. Of course you will want a Mass said for your mother,' Bella announced, as if she would be able to change the minds of the powers that be.

I left the garden as fast as I could with Leon and Rafe bouncing happily along at my side. All the way round the park I half expected the paparazzi to appear from the bushes as they had the day I'd been photographed with Philippe. The press would have a field day if they linked us with him. A murder mystery and an international footballer: the scandal sheets would love it.

Thankfully, the cooler weather meant the park was quieter; fewer people wanted to take their lunches outside in the fresh air. The leaves on the trees were beginning to turn and the air felt cool on my cheeks as I walked. I tried to work out why Bella had irritated me so much when she'd asked about Mum.

It had sounded as if she was unhappy with the press attention. If that was indeed the case, I could kind of understand her since Philippe was so often in the spotlight. But it wasn't our fault that we were front-page news; we didn't want to be in the papers any more than he did.

By the time I arrived back at Philippe's house she

seemed to be in a more conciliatory mode. She even offered me a cup of tea, which would have meant going inside. I declined the drink and hoped Charlie wouldn't flip her lid if she ever found out I'd missed a chance to infiltrate Casa Philippe. But I simply didn't feel up to sitting and making polite conversation with Bella.

Our house was quiet when I got home, so I headed for the shower. I assumed Kip had gone to Sophie's as Claude was in his cage and the computer was turned off. Perhaps once Charlie had spoken to Father O'Mara I would feel easier in my mind about recent events. He seemed like a good man and I was sure he'd give us wise advice. It would be nice if someone had wise advice to give me, especially where my love life, or the lack of it, was concerned.

16

Later that afternoon Charlie scooted in the front door. She ran straight up to change her clothes, grabbed a cereal bar from the kitchen and headed off to the florists before they closed to collect Bella's order. I put a jacket potato in the oven for her to eat later and fixed myself some noodles. Kip was still missing; I assumed he must still be with Sophie.

The evening news included the statement Philippe's solicitor had drafted with us over breakfast. A photograph of Mum filled the screen as the newscaster read out our carefully prepared speech.

'We are happy that the mystery of our mother's whereabouts has finally been solved. As a family we always believed that she would never willingly have left us. We sincerely hope that whoever took our mother's life and robbed us of her presence while we were growing up will be brought to justice so her soul can finally rest in peace.'

My noodles tasted a little saltier than usual thanks to the tears that had splashed on to my plate during the newscast. The newsreader had said the police were following new lines of inquiry. There was no mention of anything specific and I wondered how long it would be before they arrested Freddie.

Tomorrow was the deadline for returning the money we'd obtained from him and we'd heard nothing. It looked as if Charlie had been right when she'd said he was bluffing.

Philippe's solicitor had been very reassuring when we'd seen him. He'd offered to field all the requests and questions from the press, which had been a huge relief. Charlie had shouldered the responsibility for us all alone for a long time. It was nice that she finally had someone looking out for her. I just hoped she would come to her senses and become more appreciative of Philippe's kindness.

I knew she liked him but Charlie never gave her feelings away. He, on the other hand, always looked at her like a thirsty man yearning for a glass of water. Philippe was everything I'd pick if I were looking for the ideal man for Charlie. He was sexy, fit and rich, with a generous heart. I wished I could be so lucky.

A picture of Mike's face looking at me the way he'd looked when he'd kissed me goodbye only the other day swam into my mind. He hadn't been in touch since the day he'd come round to break the news about Mum.

I flicked through the TV channels in an attempt to deflect my thoughts. It was no good – not even my favourite programme about renovating run-down houses could distract me. I wondered when Kip would come home. It had started to get dark and he'd been gone for ages.

Someone knocked on the front door. I took a quick look through the window before going to answer it. I didn't recognise the man on the step but he didn't look as if he was likely to be one of Freddie's henchmen. He was slightly balding, with stooped shoulders and a worried expression on his mild-featured face, a bit like my old woodwork teacher, actually.

'I'm sorry to trouble you, but I wondered if my daughter Sophie might be here.'

His statement caught me completely off guard. 'But isn't Sophie at her home, with my brother?' My stomach did a double flip.

'No, I haven't seen either of them since lunch time. I assumed they must be here.' Sophie's father's face crumpled with fear.

'But they have to be nearby. Kip never goes out, especially not alone. He isn't good with people.' I peered wildly round Sophie's dad's shoulders as if I expected Kip to materialise out of the rapidly darkening front garden.

'When did you last see them?'

I tried to think. 'I saw Kip this morning. I went to run some errands and he was gone when I got home. I assumed he was with Sophie. He wouldn't—' I stopped short. 'I mean, I *thought* he wouldn't go anywhere else on his own . . .'

Oh God, what if Freddie's henchmen had kidnapped Kip? My lungs started to tighten and I attempted to make myself think logically.

'Come inside for a moment. I'll go and check his room.' I left Sophie's father in the hall and ran upstairs. Kip's room was in its usual untidy state. I looked around the bedside cabinet, searching by the twilight that filtered in through the window for any kind of clue as to where he might be.

Next to his model of the Starship Enterprise I spotted a folded piece of paper with my name written on it. As soon as I'd read his note I hurried back downstairs to Sophie's dad.

'They've run away!' I handed him the paper.

'Where would they go? Sophie's never done anything like this before. She's a very shy girl.' The poor man looked as upset and bewildered as I felt.

'Kip's the same. He doesn't know this area and he wouldn't go anywhere where there were lots of people.' I tried to think. 'Let me check his computer. Maybe there'll be a clue on there.'

Sophie's father followed me into the lounge, still twittering on about his daughter and suggesting we call the police. I logged on to the computer and started hunting through the search history to see if I could find anything. There were no records of Kip buying travel tickets or anything on there, but it looked as if he'd been reading up on survival techniques. My chest tightened and I started to wheeze.

'I know this is a silly question, but do you have a tent?'

Sophie's father blinked at me as I dived on my handbag for my inhaler. 'We have an old two-man tent in the garage from when Sophie was small and she went through a phase of wanting to camp in the back garden.' His face cleared as he grasped what I was driving at. 'You think that's what they're doing? Camping somewhere?'

I took two puffs from my inhaler and tried to steady my breathing. 'Maybe you should go home and check to see if the tent has gone.'

He dashed off into the night. Once the pressure on my chest had eased I looked through the notebooks that Kip kept next to the computer. Without any transport they couldn't have gone far, and Sophie appeared to be as unworldly as Kip if her father was to be believed. There hadn't been any clues in the note he'd left – only instructions on feeding and caring for his pets.

My mobile rang and I pounced on it, hoping it would be Kip letting me know he was safe.

'I hope you have the money ready for tomorrow, or you and your sister will go the same way as your car.'

The male voice cut off and I dropped the phone.

What the hell? What was wrong with the car? Charlie had the car over at the church!

I snatched my mobile up again and hit speed-dial.

'Charlie, where are you?'

I must have sounded odd. 'What's wrong? I'm just on my way out of church.'

'Where's the car?'

'In the car park. Why?'

'Don't get in it!'

'Abbey, what's going on?' Down the line I heard the muffled roar of a distant explosion and Charlie's scream.

'Charlie! Charlie!' Oh God, my heart hammered so fast I thought I would die. My mother was dead, my brother was missing, and now it sounded as if my sister had been blown up.

'The car's on fire!' It was Charlie's voice, shaky but alive. Relief that she was okay flooded through me.

I heard a flood of excited Spanish and guessed Bella must still be with her.

'Charlie!'

'I'm here. I'm okay. Oh my God, the car just blew up. I have to go.' I heard sirens wailing in the background as she cut me off.

Sophie's father reappeared at the open front door. 'You were right. The tent is missing, along with a small stove and her sleeping bag.' He looked hopefully at me, not unlike Philippe's dogs when they've returned a stick and want me to throw it again.

'Okay, we need to think. They can't have gone far.'

A big fat-bodied moth blundered in through the open door and started flapping around the hall light. Sophie's father continued to look blank.

'Let me get my shoes and a coat. I just had a thought about where they might be.' I crammed my feet into my trainers and hoped my instincts were right.

I scribbed a note for Charlie and taped it to the fridge. This was turning out to be one hell of a night. Sophie's dad had at least had the foresight to grab a torch, so we set off together towards the park.

We hadn't gone far when a familiar black sports car screeched into the street and slammed to a halt beside us.

'Abbey, are you all right?' Mike leapt from his car, leaving the door wide open in his haste to reach me. Sophie's father looked on disapprovingly as he grabbed my hands.

'Yes.' Well, I was fine, physically speaking. Mentally, I was a wreck. I didn't know who to worry over first, Charlie or Kip, and then there was the small matter of the car exploding. Freddie's men had meant what they'd said.

'We heard over the radio about an explosion in the church car park. Charlie's car registration was given out.' His face appeared haggard in the yellow street-light.

'Charlie wasn't in the car. She's okay, but that's not all. Kip is missing. He's run away.' I introduced Sophie's father.

'Do you have any idea where he might be?' Mike shut and locked his car door after picking up a flashlight from his dashboard.

'When I walked the dogs yesterday I thought I saw someone who looked like Kip on the far side of the park where it gives way to some rough ground.'

'They've taken a tent and a stove,' Sophie's father chimed in.

'Knowing Kip he wouldn't go anywhere too far away.' I hoped I was right about that.

Mike strode along beside us as we set off once more. Part of me felt pathetically grateful for his company, and a thrill of happiness that he'd been so worried when he'd heard about the car that he'd come rushing to find me. Another part of me resented the way he'd assumed I'd be happy to see him when he'd left me high and dry after formally telling me my mother was dead.

My traitorous body had no such confusion. If I hadn't been so upset about Kip and in the company of my next-door neighbour, I'd have been highly tempted to launch myself on Mike and snog his face off. How embarrassing was that?

We marched along. Sophie's father continued to

talk incessantly about his daughter while Mike made professional-sounding, soothing comments whenever there was a gap of silence. I stayed quiet and hoped my mobile would ring with a message from either Charlie or Kip.

I mulled over the contents of Kip's note in my head as we walked. Apart from the pet care instructions it had said that Sophie didn't want to go to college and he thought Charlie and I would be better off if he wasn't at home any more. I assumed he felt he was to blame for our life of crime since Charlie and I had pulled off the scams to make money for him.

With the latest turn of events – Mum's body being found and Freddie hounding us for his money – Kip must have felt it was all somehow his fault. I knew he'd been worried that Charlie and I would be arrested. Poor Kip, I should have paid more attention to how all this was affecting him.

The streetlights ended and the park loomed before us, dark and scary. In the distance dogs barked and the trees made a whooshing, shooshing sound as the leaves shivered in the breeze. I crept a step closer to Mike.

'Where did you think you saw him?' Mike shone his torch into the darkness.

'On the very far side of the lake, past the band of trees that marks the edge of the park. The dogs ran off there the other day and I had to go and chase them out. It looked as if other people had made fires and dens there.' I shivered a little as a gust of wind tugged at my hair.

'Do you know this area well?' Mike turned to Sophie's dad.

'Not really. Sophie never liked to go out very much and now she's a teenager we never have any call to come to the park any more. Not that we ever came much.'

I sensed rather than heard Mike's sigh of exasperation. Sophie's father seemed about as much use as a chocolate teapot.

'Then we'd better follow the path till we reach the lake. Abbey, do you think you can guide us from there?' Mike asked.

'Yes, I think so.'

'Good girl.'

The approval in his voice helped lift my spirits. Sophie's dad switched on his torch and we entered the tunnel of trees that led deeper into the heart of the park. The combined light from the flashlights picked out the tarmac path in front of us, making alien shapes of the landscape. Above our heads the trees continued to murmur and whisper, breaking the silence that surrounded us as we walked.

The eyes of some animal flashed yellow-green in the light from the torch and I let out a yelp as a cat shot across in front of us. Mike's hand found mine, warm and reassuring as my pulse settled back down into a slightly less erratic beat. Even simply having him hold my hand sent flickers of desire racing through my veins.

We reached the end of the path and the field with the pool opened up before us. The light from the torches didn't extend very far over the grass and clouds scudded across the surface of the half-moon above our heads. I could barely make out the glimmer of the water's surface and the huddled, sleeping shapes of the lakeside geese.

'Watch where you're walking. The ground is quite uneven,' Mike warned us.

Sophie's father promptly tripped over a tussock of grass, recovering his balance at the last minute. I directed us across the open ground towards the straggly unkempt trees and bushes that fringed the far side of the field.

'Should we call for them?' I whispered to Mike. The sibilant silence of the darkness that surrounded us felt eerie.

'Go ahead,' he answered in his normal voice, squeezing my hand in reassurance.

'Kip! Sophie!' We roamed amongst the trees calling their names. Sophie's father limped along beside us adding his shouts to ours. The geese honked disapprovingly from the water's edge as we made our way further out of the cultivated area and into the scrubby wilderness.

A flash of blue man-made material caught my

attention as Mike played the torchlight around the search area.

'Over there!' I grabbed his arm and we stumbled as fast as we could towards the material I'd seen. Sophie's dad puffed along behind us.

We broke through the bushes to discover the camp. An empty blue two-man pup tent was erected in a small clearing. Scattered on the ground were two half-empty tubs of Pot Noodle and a torch. It looked as if we'd interrupted their meal.

'Christopher Michael Gifford, get out here now!' I knew Kip couldn't be far away.

We waited next to the tent. The branches of a bush opposite parted as Mike played the light from his torch on to the leaves. Kip's tousled auburn head appeared and he emerged from his hiding place followed by a small, scared-looking blond-haired girl.

'Sophie!' Her father rushed forward to scoop his errant daughter into an awkward embrace.

'Are we in trouble?' Kip stood to one side and twisted his baseball cap between his fingers.

'Too bloody right you are.' I hugged him tight, too grateful to have found him safe and sound to tell him off right at that moment. I knew I could safely leave that task to Charlie.

17

Charlie was waiting on the front doorstep when we made our sorry way home. I was enormously relieved she was in one piece. I don't know what I would do if I ever lost my sister. Sophie and her father made a sharp turn towards their house, while Kip and I braced ourselves to meet Hurricane Charlie. Mike had held my hand all the way back from the park while Kip had skulked moodily alongside us.

Sophie's father had talked constantly to his daughter all the way home, so the rest of us had stayed silent during his litany of hurts. After listening to him I began to understand why Sophie had run away.

Charlie's eyes were red-rimmed from crying and her normally immaculate face looked blotched and puffy. Philippe hovered anxiously in the background, obviously concerned at her distress.

'Get upstairs and go to bed.' She released Kip from the stranglehold hug that she'd launched on him the minute he'd set foot over the step. 'I'm too tired and upset to talk to you tonight.'

Kip took her at her word and fled up to his room, relieved to have a small reprieve from the storm to come. Mike and I followed her and Philippe into the lounge.

'How are you, Charlie?' I unfastened my jacket and dropped it on Kip's computer chair before giving her a hug.

She dropped on to the sofa, her slim frame quivering with suppressed emotion. 'How do you think I am? The car is totalled and I get home to find the house empty and Kip missing.'

Philippe slipped his arm around her and murmured something in Spanish that sounded soothing.

'What happened with the car? The report mentioned an incendiary device.' Mike took a seat opposite Philippe and Charlie. I swallowed hard and prayed he wouldn't ask me anything.

Charlie shrugged. 'I don't know. I was talking to Abbey on my mobile as I came out of church and then, bang, my car blew up. We've been receiving threatening phone calls, as you know, and I assume this was the same person taking those threats one step further.'

Philippe didn't appear shocked by Charlie's statement so I assumed she must have told him some kind of story to account for the threats. She was hardly likely to have told him the truth.

Mike looked at me. 'Is that true, Abbey?'

'Yes. There have been a few more calls since the first one.' *Oh, hell, please don't let him ask me anything else.*

'Okay.' He turned back to Charlie and started asking her some more questions about the explosion. I slipped off to the kitchen and made a pot of tea. Thank heavens he hadn't dug any deeper with his line of questioning or it would all have come out – Freddie's threats, the scam, the money, everything.

We probably wouldn't have seen Philippe for dust and I suspected the only handholding Mike would have wanted to do with me would have involved a set of handcuffs. I knew Mike suspected we'd been up to something but there had to be a limit on how much he could ignore. Somehow, I thought extortion and fraud would be well over the line.

I carried the tray through into the lounge.

'Charlie, I do not think you should remain here in this house while this man is around. Mike, you are the police, can you not arrest him?' Philippe sounded quite agitated as I handed out mugs of tea.

'That was partly why I was here tonight. I had been planning to come and update Abbey and Charlie on the progress of the investigation when I got news of the explosion.' Mike spooned sugar into his mug. I didn't think Mike took sugar; this had to be something bad.

I took a seat on the spare armchair. 'Are you planning to arrest Freddie?'

Mike stirred his tea and carefully placed the spoon down on the tray. 'Since we recovered your mother's body and confirmed identification we've been working on establishing the cause of death, seeking out witnesses, reviewing past records et cetera, all of this with a view to finding the culprit and bringing charges against him.'

'And? How did she die?' Charlie asked.

Mike sighed. 'I'm sorry, Charlie. Your mum's cause of death has now been established as a single gunshot wound to the head.'

My hand jerked involuntarily, spilling my tea on to my fingers. I put the mug down and grabbed at some tissues to mop up the burning fluid.

'I'm sorry, Abbey. I warned you there wasn't an easy way to tell you any of this. I know it's all a terrible shock.' Mike's voice was gentle as I sucked at the scalded spot on the back of my hand. His eyes held such heartfelt compassion when he looked at me that I felt my heart rate pick up.

'You have the evidence now to bring the charges against the man who did this crime?' Philippe stroked Charlie's hair as she leaned against him, her face pale next to the dark grey of his jacket.

'We do. My colleague, Diane, was set to formally charge Freddie Davis with the murder of your mother and the other man found in the grave with her. We have evidence linking him to the weapon that was used as well as other material that implicates him in the murders.'

All three of us stared at Mike, trying to comprehend what he was saying.

'Your colleague *was set*? What happened?' Charlie asked what we were all thinking.

'Freddie's done a runner.' Mike grimaced as he took a mouthful of his drink.

The tiny amount of tea I'd consumed swirled and boiled around in my stomach.

'Then Charlie is not safe, or is Kip and Abbey. This man, he is dangerous and he has the fixation with Charlie. She needs protection.' Philippe's English became more scrambled in his concern for my sister's safety. 'This man, he has tried to murder Charlie.'

'I agree. Maybe you should all consider moving to a safe house for a while,' Mike suggested.

'No, we couldn't. Kip would find it really hard to cope,' Charlie protested.

Her fears mirrored my own. Our life here had been so good, so settled, so normal, and for the first time ever I'd felt we had a future. That we could finally live the way other people did, and have jobs, friends, boyfriends . . . Freddie had robbed us of our mother – he wasn't going to rob us of our dreams too.

'But you are not safe. This man, he is a lunatic.' Philippe looked horrified by Charlie's refusal to consider moving.

'Did you receive any kind of threat just before the car exploded?' Mike asked, looking at me once more and knowing I was powerless to do anything other than tell him the truth.

'Yes. That's why I rang Charlie at the church.' Crap. I did not want to have to tell him all of this.

'What was the nature of the threat?' Mike's eyes were steely and I knew he was angry that I hadn't given him all the information when he'd first asked about the explosion.

'There was a phone call. A man, not Freddie. He said Charlie and I would get the same treatment as the car.'

Tension hung in the air and Charlie's eyes widened in alarm.

'You see, the man, this Freddie, he is mad!' Philippe circled a pointed finger near his temple in the universal signal for lunacy.

Mike continued to look at me and I prayed he wouldn't ask anything else. One more question and we would be done for.

'If you won't agree to move then we will have to look at protecting you here, at least until Freddie has been arrested, and with the current level of manpower that may prove difficult to facilitate.' Mike didn't sound happy.

'We can't move.' Charlie was defiant.

'It's too risky for you to stay here. I can't guarantee

that we will be able to provide the right level of protection.' Mike sounded as stubborn as my sister.

Philippe dug inside his Armani jacket and pulled out his mobile. 'I will arrange private security for Charlie. I will make some calls.'

'Excuse me! Don't I have some say in this?' Charlie extricated herself from Philippe's embrace.

Mike ignored Charlie's outburst and answered Philippe. 'That might not be such a bad idea. I can arrange surveillance for the house in case Freddie shows up here, if you could arrange for the girls to have some security if they go out.'

'What?' Charlie looked furious but Philippe had already hit speed-dial. She started to protest but he held up his hand to silence her while launching into a flood of Spanish with whoever had answered his call.

'Is all arranged. They arrive here early in the morning.' Philippe slid his phone shut and smiled at Charlie. She folded her arms and looked sulky.

'I'd better inform my team of the latest developments. There'll be someone posted to watch the house until Philippe's people get here. I'll arrange for you all to have personal alarms. Abbey, if you receive any more phone calls or texts you will tell me immediately, is that understood?' Mike didn't sound as if he would take any messing.

'Okay.'

Charlie glowered at me from the sofa.

'Good, that's settled then. I don't think Freddie will try anything if the girls are accompanied. With any luck we should be able to pick him up soon.' Mike finished his mug of tea.

'Fabulous. Can't wait.' Charlie looked as if the milk in her tea had turned sour.

Philippe kissed her on the lips. 'I want to make sure you are safe. You are *muy* important to me.'

I felt quite mushy at the tenderness on his face when he looked at my sister. It would have been nice to see a trace of that same kind of affection in Mike's expression when he looked at me, but in contrast at the moment he just appeared faintly exasperated.

Charlie disappeared into the hall to see Philippe out. Mike settled down, opened his phone and began to text as if he planned to spend all night in our armchair.

'Shouldn't you be out looking for Freddie?'

Mike raised an eyebrow and carried on hitting buttons on his phone.

'I didn't think Philippe's hiring private security would have been something you approved of.' I was determined to get a response from him. His laid-back attitude and the way he'd just popped back into my life as if he'd never been away was really irritating me. I was glad he was around but I still felt confused about what he might feel for me, or me for him come to think of it.

He finished his messaging and returned his

phone to his pocket. 'Under normal circumstances you might be right.'

I folded my arms and tried to look bored.

'Are you going to tell me the parts you left out about Charlie's car blowing up?'

I stared at him.

'I know you have to tell me the truth. What did you leave out, Abbey?'

'Freddie wants money.' Double crap. My hands flew to cover my mouth but it was too late.

Mike leaned forward in his seat. 'How much money?'

I tried clenching my teeth to keep the answer in. 'Thirty thousand pounds.'

'I know I'm going to regret this,' Mike muttered. 'Abbey, why does Freddie want thirty thousand pounds from you and Charlie?'

'Because that's how much we scammed him for.' I closed my eyes and waited to feel the inevitable clap of steel on my wrists.

Nothing happened. No clap of thunder, no reading of my rights.

I peeped at Mike from between my eyelashes. What I saw broke my heart.

'I take it this wasn't the first time you've pulled a scam?' His eyes were hard and cold.

'No.' It was almost a relief to have everything out in the open. Except the look on Mike's face told me that whatever he had been expecting me to confess to, this was much worse. His words confirmed my worst fears.

'For someone who can't lie you have a very strange relationship with the truth. I'd guessed you two were up to something but I didn't realise how much. Maybe someone should be warning Philippe just what he's got himself into by letting your sister play him for a sucker. Or is that what you've been doing to me too?' His voice was icy. 'Don't bother to answer that, Abbey. I think I can guess.' With that, he got to his feet and strode out of the room, pushing past Charlie as she came back in.

'Abbey?'

I couldn't answer her. Instead, I bolted for the safety of my room, devastated.

I didn't sleep. For what was left of the night I tossed and turned, wondering if Mike would come back with a team of uniformed policemen to arrest me and Charlie. I had nightmares about him telling Philippe that we were con women and that he should stay away from us. Charlie's heart would be broken and everything would be messed up.

By the time I staggered downstairs to the kitchen for breakfast the next day there were two large foreign-looking men in tight black T-shirts encamped in our lounge. I wrapped my dressing gown a little tighter around me, muttered good morning and scuttled past them to get to the cornflakes in the kitchen.

'Who are they?' I hissed to Kip.

'Philippe's private security men. They got here an hour ago. They don't speak much English.' He scooped a spoonful of cereal from his bowl and stared morosely through the window at the garden. Outside the weather looked damp and drizzly – as miserable as my mood.

'Have you seen Charlie?' The cornflake packet felt suspiciously light. I up-ended it and six flakes fell into my dish. It was a good thing I hadn't much appetite.

He glowered at me. 'I had a huge lecture this morning and she says I can't see Sophie any more.'

'Well, what did you expect her to say? You frightened us half to death with that stunt you pulled last night.' I gave up on the cereal.

'Dunno. I was looking after Sophie. Besides, it's not fair if you and Charlie get in trouble just because you want to buy me a farm.' He poked at his breakfast with his spoon.

'If Charlie and I get in trouble it won't be because of you. It'll be because of me.'

Kip stopped prodding at his cornflakes and stared at me. 'You look terrible. What do you mean, if you get in trouble it's because of you?'

'Mike knows.' Which was more than Charlie did. I'd been too upset to talk to her last night. She'd knocked on my bedroom door but I couldn't bring myself to answer.

'Knows what?' Kip put down his spoon and sat up straighter at the breakfast bar.

'Everything. Absolutely everything about Freddie, about the money, the scam – everything.'

Kip gaped at me. 'What's he going to do? Are you and Charlie going to go to prison?'

'I don't know. He slammed out of here last night after I told him. He looked so angry.' My voice wobbled and I delved in my dressing-gown pocket for a tissue. 'I don't know if he plans to tell Philippe.'

'He knows about Charlie's plans for robbing Philippe?'

'No, not that. He's guessed that Charlie isn't just dating Philippe because she likes him, though.'

Kip fidgeted on his stool and placed a clumsy hand on my shoulder. 'It'll be okay, Abbey.'

I wished I could believe him. 'It's over between me and Mike. The only way he's likely to want to see me again is if he can read me a charge sheet, and if he tells Philippe what he suspects, then Charlie will be busted too.' I tried not to cry; my nose and eyes felt sore enough already from the tears I'd shed in the night.

'Why will I be busted?' Charlie entered the kitchen.

'Mike knows all about the scams. I don't know what he's going to tell Philippe.' I repeated everything that had happened the previous night. It would be pointless to try to delay telling Charlie.

Her face paled and she sank down on to the spare stool next to Kip.

'Okay, in that case we need to make a plan.' She took a deep breath and squared her shoulders. Then, together, we held a Gifford family crisis meeting in the kitchen.

Fortunately, our security *hombres* appeared to be happily occupied watching the Teletubbies in the lounge while we sat at the breakfast bar in the kitchen and Charlie ran through our options.

'Option A – we sit tight, do nothing, and wait and see what happens. With any luck this could all blow over.'

'Do you think that's likely?' Mike had looked so angry when he'd left; I couldn't see that he'd be content to sit back and do nothing. He knew we were criminals now so surely he had to take some course of action as a man of the law.

'Maybe. It's quite possible. After all, he hasn't done anything yet, and let's be honest here – it's only your word. You have been hit by lightning, so . . .' She quirked her shoulders in an optimistic shrug.

Great, so I'm a fruit and nut job.

'Charlie has a point, Abbey. I could get some medical evidence from the Net and tell him you were delusional.' Kip's eyes lit up with enthusiasm.

I couldn't believe the two of them. They would

rather pretend I was bonkers than admit I was honest if it meant we'd escape being charged. The man I'd fallen in love with would be convinced I was a fantasist who'd imagined all those memories from my childhood and hallucinated my 'truth'. I didn't know which would be worse: Mike thinking I was a crook or Mike thinking I was mad.

'What are the other options?' I folded my arms and glared at them.

'Option B – we go to Mike and confess everything. I come clean with Philippe and we take the consequences. I'll plead mitigating circumstances, like Kip's Rain Man tendencies and your lightning strike, and chances are we'd get off quite lightly. Maybe even a community sentence.'

'Or we'd get sectioned,' I muttered.

Now it was Kip's turn to glare at her. 'What do you mean, Rain Man tendencies?'

'Philippe would never forgive you.' I added my four penn'orth to the mix and hoped Kip would forget Charlie's comment.

I saw her swallow and bite her lip. 'Well, from what you said about Mike's reaction, I suppose Philippe's likely to hear something bad about me anyway.'

'I do not have Rain Man tendencies.' Kip picked at the rim of the breakfast bar and continued to glower at Charlie.

'What other options do we have?' I ignored Kip's

muttering. I knew Charlie really cared for Philippe, even if she didn't show it much in public, and to tell him what would almost certainly finish things between them would be very painful for her.

'Option C – we go to Mike and come up with a plan to lure Freddie out into the open. It would make it harder for them to press charges against us if we cooperated with them in catching a really hardened criminal, and if they did it would go in our favour. I'd pre-empt Mike and talk to Philippe.' I guessed she meant that she'd give Philippe her own spin on why we'd moved up north and why she'd sought him out.

Of all the options she'd mentioned that one sounded the best so far.

'Any other ideas?' Kip asked.

'We give the guards the slip and make a run for it, start somewhere else under a new identity.'

Now who was bonkers?

'What, move abroad or something? We don't have passports. I don't want to go on a plane, Charlie.' Kip stared at her. I could see he had started to panic. I had visions of us having to drug him.

'Charlie's kidding with that suggestion.' I kicked her ankle under the breakfast bar.

'Yeah, just kidding.' She scowled at me. I guess I must have kicked her a little harder than I'd intended.

'That's good. I don't know if Claude and Stig would have liked flying, either.' Kip appeared relieved.

In the lounge we could hear the sound of the Teletubbies theme tune, signalling the end of the programme.

'Okay then, which one are we going for? We have to make a decision,' Charlie said.

I have to say I didn't care for any of them much. I'd rather have gone for my preferred option – option Z – where we would ask Kip to invent a time machine to take us back to before everything went wrong.

'I think you should tell Philippe the truth and tell him how you feel.' Kip traced a pattern in some spilled milk on the surface of the breakfast bar. 'You've been going to church and everything so he'd believe you were a good person inside, especially if you were really sorry.'

Kip had a point. Philippe adored Charlie. Maybe if she came clean and threw herself on his mercy he would forgive her. She did like Philippe, maybe even loved him, and surely that had to count for something.

Charlie didn't look as if she thought that idea was very appealing. 'What do we do about Freddie? And the possibility of Mike arresting me and Abbey?'

'Set a trap, like you said.' Kip looked up from his milk pattern. 'Freddie must be desperate for the money so he can get away. If we pretend to give it to him then the police could catch him and you and Abbey would be heroines.'

He made it all sound so simple.

'What do you reckon, Abbey? If I talk to Philippe, will you talk to Mike?' Charlie asked.

I didn't know if Mike would listen to anything I said but I supposed it had to be worth a try. His opinion of me couldn't get any lower and even if everything was over between us at least this way he might think I wasn't all bad.

I made the security *hombres* a drink while Charlie left a message on Philippe's mobile asking him to call round to the house after training.

Kip went out into the damp garden. He claimed it was to check up on our security at the back of the house, but I suspected it was to try to spot Sophie up at her bedroom window. From what he'd told me, Sophie's father had grounded her too as her punishment for running away.

I took my phone up to my room and tried to figure out what to say to Mike. My heart hammered in my chest while I tried to pluck up the courage to call. Finally I took a deep breath and forced my reluctant fingers to press the digits.

Voice mail – bloody typical. 'Mike, please call me, there's something urgent I need to tell you.' I rang off, feeling sick and shaky now the deed was done.

Father O'Mara called round at lunch time to discuss arranging a Mass for Mum. I let him into the hall feeling guilty for every bad thing we'd ever done. The service was booked for Monday afternoon at the church. He said he would mention it in the notices after Mass on Sunday so that a few more people might attend to support us.

After he'd gone, we ate lunch with the security men and waited for Philippe to arrive. Charlie took him up to her room the minute he stepped through the door. I headed for the lounge with Kip. We sat together in silence pretending to be interested in an old episode of *Murder, She Wrote* until we heard the front door slam followed by the sound of Charlie's feet running back upstairs.

'How do you think it went?' Kip asked.

'Badly.'

My mobile rang, making me jump. I dived on it, hoping it would show Mike's caller ID, but instead I heard another male voice. One I would have preferred not to hear.

'I hope you and your bitch of a sister have got my money.'

'Who is this?' I knew full well who it was but I wasn't sure if my phone was tapped.

'Don't play games with me. I want that money. Tell Lady Charlotte to meet me tonight outside that church she seems so bloody fond of. Ten o'clock and no police.'

'What if we don't have the money?' Oh God, what the hell were we going to do?

'I suggest you damn well get it. You saw what happened to the car.' He sounded irritated and I pictured his ruddy face reddening with temper.

'And my mother?' The words popped out unbidden.

There was a moment's silence.

'Eulalie was a fool. An interfering, bloody fool. She thought she was clever too, just like you and your sister. Ten o'clock, or else.' He rang off.

Kip's freckles stood out in stark relief on the chalky whiteness of his face. He'd been watching and listening. 'Freddie?' he croaked.

'He wants us to take the money to the church tonight.' Visions of a darkened graveyard danced in front of my eyes and I felt my lungs twinge. I needed to go and get my asthma prescription reviewed.

Kip glanced in the direction of the half-open kitchen door. The Spaniards were playing cards at the breakfast bar. 'What are we going to do?'

'I don't know. We'd better go and tell Charlie.'

She opened her door on our third knock. Her red eyes and puffy face told their own story of how things had gone with Philippe. We filled her in on the latest phone call.

'Have you spoken to Mike?' she asked me.

'I had to leave a voice mail. I told him it was urgent.'

She nibbled at the corner of one of her acrylic nail extensions while she thought about what to do next. 'This is the ideal opportunity to catch Freddie.'

'This isn't the movies, Charlie. He could have a

gun or anything. Plus, how do we manage to get out of the house without the Spanish inquisition coming with us? He did say no police.'

She rolled her eyes. 'They *always* say no police. Typical Freddie, no originality ... He murdered Mum. We have to catch him.'

'I could get Sophie to set up a diversion,' Kip suggested.

We looked at him, both in equal surprise.

'I've got some chemicals and stuff. I could set up a flash and smoke display in the back garden and then we could dash out the front. Sophie could do some screaming so they would think you were outside.' He looked really pleased with himself.

'I thought Sophie had been grounded?' Charlie lifted an enquiring eyebrow.

The tips of Kip's ears turned pink. 'We worked out a signalling system with mirrors and torches.'

Charlie sighed. 'But then how do we trap him? Abbey has a point – he might not be alone and he might have a gun or something. He killed Mum and Harry, so I don't think it would bother him too much if he had to kill us too. He's not likely to want to leave any witnesses.'

'If Mike rings back, we could get the police to set up a back-up to catch him when you go to the churchyard.'

My suggestion was met with scorn by my sister.

'Do you think the police would be willing to let us

go ahead with something so risky? They would want to replace us with policewomen and Freddie would smell a rat straight away.'

Maybe she had a point.

'I still think we should tell him,' I said. 'We need help.'

Charlie had always been a bit gung-ho. She'd always been the one to take the risks; I was more cautious in my outlook.

'Maybe.' She didn't sound convinced.

'I've got a plan!' Kip was positively bouncing in his cross-legged position on Charlie's bed.

We listened to his idea and, somewhat surprisingly, it made sense. Sort of. Okay, so maybe it didn't, but it was all we had and it was no madder than some of the scams we'd pulled. Once we'd ironed out some of the details we trotted off to make our various individual preparations: Kip to play with his chemicals, Charlie to hunt through her underwear drawer looking for a weapon and me to find a costume.

I pulled my box of wigs and stage make-up from the back of my wardrobe with a sense of foreboding. When I'd stuffed them behind my selection of costume pieces I'd hoped that I'd never need them again.

One third of my closet was given over to props. They were all garments I'd acquired from various charity shops and jumble sales for the different scams that we'd pulled. I had old-lady cardigans, tweed skirts, business suits and dippy hippy-chick boho skirts. I hated all of them.

Because of those clothes, and who I became when I wore them, I'd lost the one guy I'd ever allowed myself to become fond of. Who was I kidding? I was more than fond of Mike. A part of me had hoped that I might have had a future with him, a normal future with a house and maybe even a family. Was that crazy after I'd only known him for a few weeks? Maybe, but there had been a connection between us that had felt so strong that I'd been carried along with my daydreams.

I couldn't believe he hadn't called me back. When his car had screeched to a halt next to me last night and I'd seen the concern in his eyes when he thought I might have been blown up, then I'd been sure he cared about me the way I cared for him.

The way I loved him.

Crap. I was in more trouble than I thought. That had all been before he'd seen the real me. The con artist and crook. Why would he care about me? He probably wasn't even sure who the real me actually was. Until recently I hadn't been sure who the real me was either. Meeting Mike and moving north had altered all that but it looked as if it was too late to make a difference.

I cooked tea and we watched the soaps with the bodyguards. They seemed pleasant enough if you liked large foreign men with limited English and overdeveloped biceps. I'd half expected them to leave after Charlie's conversation with Philippe but although he might not want to see her again he clearly didn't want her to be murdered either.

Charlie faked a yawn and announced her intentions of a bath and an early night. Kip remained in the lounge to keep the Spaniards busy while I slipped off upstairs to get changed into my disguise.

'And tonight, Matthew, I'm going to play a sweet little old granny,' I muttered as I stared critically at my reflection in the floor-length mirror of my built-in wardrobe. A grey curly wig, floral skirt, collared blouse and cardigan effected my transformation. Over my arm hung a Marks and Spencer shopping bag and I'd completed the image with plain glasses and stage make-up. I looked freakily like Aunty Beatrice. I took a couple of puffs from my inhaler for good luck and waited for the signal.

Sure enough, at nine o'clock a huge bang shook the house and Sophie started screeching like a scalded cat from her garden. I bolted down the stairs right behind Charlie and we snuck through the smoke-filled hall and out of the front door. We could already hear cursing in both English and Spanish coming from the direction of the back garden.

Once clear of the street we slowed our pace. I swiped a bunch of dahlias from someone's front garden and stuffed them in the top of my shopping bag as I hobbled past. They were to form part of my disguise when I got to the graveyard. Charlie parted company from me two streets before the church and I went ahead alone.

My pulse hammered in my throat as I slowly made my way along the main road to the churchyard. I focused on limping along with my shoulders bent, muttering to myself as I walked. I fished the purloined dahlias from my shopper. With any luck, to the casual passer-by I'd appear to be some batty old dear on her way to put flowers on a grave late at night.

However, I also had in my old-lady shopping bag my mobile, a can of hairspray, and a taser. Charlie had acquired the taser about a year ago from a bloke in a pub when she'd thought we might be getting into some dodgy deals. I wasn't certain that I'd be able to use it but I did feel safer knowing it was there. The hairspray was for extra back-up.

I supposed there weren't many things I would do in life that were likely to be dodgier than meeting a known murderer in a churchyard at night. Quaking in my granny shoes, I made my way muttering and mumbling in the gloomy darkness along the path between the graves towards the church.

The earlier drizzle of the day had given way to a
damp September evening. Just the sort of
weather you wanted if you planned to spend a few
hours in a churchyard with a murderer. The church
itself was lit at the front by a yellow footlight which
threw the façade and spire into relief against the
cloudy night sky. The blue and white painted figure
of Our Lady eyed me reproachfully from her spot
near the west doors of the church.

I slowly made my way along the path, shuffling
my feet and clutching my stolen dahlias, keeping a
sharp look out for any sign of movement from
amongst the shadows. I had no idea of the precise
location where Freddie wanted Charlie to meet him
within the churchyard. Knowing our luck, it would
be the darkest corner where the grass cuttings were
tipped and the dead flowers lay on the compost.

Charlie and I had swapped phones so Freddie
could call her with instructions. She would then
hopefully text me so I would know where she was. I
wondered how Kip had coped with the fallout from

his smoke and sparks bomb. The bodyguards and the police would be a bit upset when they realised Charlie and I were missing.

I selected a random grave near the top of the slope that looked as if it were short of some loving care and began to tidy it up. It had a good view of most of the graves but was itself hidden behind another crumbly box-style tombstone. Apparently, the grave belonged to a James Donohue, born in 1927 and died in 1982, resting in the arms of the Lord.

Poor Mr Donohue. Unlike his neighbours he didn't appear to have had any family; there were no names of a loving wife or children engraved after him on his stone. I filled the little posy bowl on the grave with fresh water from the standpipe on the edge of the path and crouched down to arrange my purloined dahlias. The church itself stood a few rows away from me at the top of a small hill. The rest of the graveyard fell away towards the road and the car park.

A movement in the inky blackness on the far side of the graves caught my eye. I carefully shuffled round so that I couldn't be seen by whoever lurked near the yew trees in the bottom corner where the oldest graves lay forlorn and neglected in the dark. The clouds which had been covering the moon shifted, revealing a man's bulky figure waiting next to a stone angel. My heart started to race.

I knelt down on the cold, wet grass next to the grave and texted Charlie.

He's here.

My watch said ten to ten. I watched from my vantage point next to the late Mr Donohue's stone as Freddie pulled out his phone and dialled. The blue screen of his mobile glowed luminous in the shadows. I guessed he must be calling my phone. If our plan had worked so far, Charlie would be loitering at a bus stop five minutes away, ready to make her entrance.

Sure enough, after a few more minutes I saw Charlie's tall, slim figure walk along the road and approach the wooden gates at the cemetery entrance. The amber street lamps fringing the perimeter wall picked out her dark hair and pale blue jacket. She disappeared for a moment as she entered the lychgate before becoming visible once more as she started her ascent along the gloomy graveyard path.

Her heels tapped on the tarmac as she drew nearer to my hiding place. I froze behind the gravestone. It was important that Freddie didn't spot me. If she came too close to me at this point the plan would turn into a disaster and we would both be in danger. My chest tightened and I forced myself to concentrate on my breathing. I had no intention of being murdered because of my asthma.

A couple of rows before my hiding place she turned away and headed along a smaller path that ran round the church in a kind of loop. I wiggled my shoulders to release a bit of the tension and looked for Freddie. The place where he'd been standing was empty.

Crap. I couldn't afford to lose him now. I needed to be able to sneak up behind him while Charlie held his attention. Everything depended on my being in the right place at the right time. I had to rely on the element of surprise if we were to disable him with the taser until the police could get to us.

I bent down and scuttled as quietly as I could to another stone. My efforts were rewarded by a glimpse of Freddie's camel-coloured coat near the rubbish heap. Charlie was right – the man wasn't very original. I would have placed money on that being his chosen spot for the rendezvous.

Charlie paused on the path as though peering around to get her bearings. Now I knew where she was headed I inched my way, crab-like, in the opposite direction so I could get behind Freddie. She needed to stall her meeting until I'd had time to get round the building.

I'd underestimated the darkness at the rear of the church. The ground was steeper and the grass rougher as I tried to pick my way quietly through the graves. Fortunately, it sounded as if the local pub had a live band playing and the faint sounds of guitars and drumming helped mask my noisy movements.

I had Charlie in my sights again. She was pretending to be a bit ditzy and confused as she picked her way towards the compost heap. Freddie was in deep shadow, with his back to me. I carefully crept closer and closer until I was within five gravestones of his position.

'Where's the money?' His voice made me jump.

'In my bag. Where are you? I can't see you.' Charlie's voice wobbled slightly, betraying her nerves.

'Come closer,' Freddie commanded.

I extracted the taser from my bag and curled my fingers round it before abandoning my shopper behind a stone cross dedicated to Nellie Murphy, sadly missed by her loving husband Neville.

Charlie walked a few paces closer to where Freddie waited like a big fat spider in the darkness. Blood pounded in my ears as she drew nearer.

'Stop there.' Freddie stepped out of the shadows to face my sister.

The two of them stared at one another. Time appeared to stand still.

'Get the money out and put it on the floor.'

Charlie opened her fake Burberry bag.

'No tricks.' He shifted and I saw the glint of metal in his hand as the moonlight broke through the clouds again, illuminating the scene.

Charlie pulled out a big brown envelope, which she placed on the grass in front of her. I gripped the taser and tried to remember how I was supposed to use it. I wasn't even certain that it actually worked. I mean, it wasn't the kind of thing you could test on anyone. Kip had said it knocked people unconscious. I just hoped he was right.

'The money's in the envelope.' Charlie lifted her chin. Now all she needed to do was keep Freddie occupied while I crept close enough to knock him out.

'It had better be.' Freddie lifted his gun and pointed it at Charlie.

Shit.

I took aim and pulled the trigger on the taser.

Nothing.

Memories of my mother and how she'd died flashed through my mind. That miserable piece of scum had killed my mum. He wasn't going to murder my sister. I launched myself from my hiding place with a scream and connected with his back. Freddie swore and jerked round, throwing me loose so that I landed on the grass with a thump. The taser disappeared into the pile of rotting grass cuttings and dead flowers.

I struggled to get my breath. My ribs and knees hurt from the force of my landing on the rough ground. Already I could feel dampness from the dew oozing up off the grass through my granny skirt to wet my bum. That would teach us to buy an illegal weapon from a bloke in a pub; we should have guessed it was a fake.

Freddie twirled round like a grotesquely overweight ballet dancer, his gun wavering alternately between Charlie and me.

'What the hell is going on?' He stared at me.

I suppose getting attacked by what appeared to be a little old lady probably hadn't figured in his list of potential problems when he'd set off earlier this evening to collect the money from Charlie.

'Don't move.' He whirled back round to point the gun at Charlie, who had stepped forward in an attempt to get to me.

'This is consecrated ground, sonny!' I wailed in my best impersonation of Aunty Beatrice. Maybe if I convinced him that I really was a passing old lady then Charlie and I might escape. I was pretty sure he hadn't even seen the taser. We might have a problem, though, if he saw through the stage make-up and recognised Lady Charlotte's rather inept personal assistant.

'Take what you came for and go.' Charlie looked terrified but continued to look Freddie right in the eyes.

'Attacking a defenceless young woman. You should be ashamed of yourself!' I added as Freddie continued to divide his attention between us, an expression of complete bewilderment on his face.

In the distance I heard a siren wailing. God, I hoped it was the cavalry on its way.

'Get up, you interfering old biddy.' Freddie waved the gun at me.

I levered myself on to my knees and made a big deal of heaving myself up to my feet, my mind working like crazy as I tried to figure out a new plan of escape.

Freddie grimaced. His ruddy features creased in pain and he rubbed at the centre of his chest with his free hand. 'Over there, with her.' He motioned at me with the gun to go and stand next to Charlie.

'Disgusting, that's what it is.' I hobbled over to my sister. I wondered what was wrong with him; he seemed to be suffering some kind of chest pain.

'This is a churchyard. No respect at all.' I mumbled and sucked my teeth.

My hip hurt from my fall, which – ironically – made my performance as the old lady that little bit more convincing. If I survived I suspected I'd have a big bruise running down the side of my thigh.

Freddie gave a funny little stagger. His complexion appeared to turn grey in the poor light as he clutched at his chest.

His gun went off with a strange whiny sound. The bullet missed us by a good six feet and took out a chunk of a marble angel's wing with a loud bang as a tombstone shattered. I grabbed at the front of my sister's jacket.

Freddie made a strange gargling noise in his throat.

'What the hell are you doing?' Charlie screamed at him.

Freddie fell on to his knees. The gun wavered in his hand as he pointed it at us once more. My feet were glued to the spot. I couldn't move even though my brain told me I needed to run. Charlie gave me a hard shove sideways while at the same time she dived to the floor in the opposite direction.

The gun fired once again, the bullet pinging off another headstone with a loud crack. Freddie made a croaking noise and collapsed on top of the grave of Arthur Smith, who departed this life on the fifteenth of October, 1899.

I lay still on the grass, too scared to move in case it was some kind of trick.

Charlie crawled on her knees to a safe place behind another gravestone. 'Freddie?' She called his name and peeped out over the top.

He remained where he'd fallen.

'What the hell are you doing?' I couldn't believe she was trying to rouse the man who'd just attempted to shoot us. It looked as if he'd had some kind of coronary.

'Are you okay?' She looked across at me, her eyes huge against the pallor of her face.

I nodded. Freddie still lay motionless like some macabre dummy, half draped over the heart-shaped marble tombstone.

'Do you think he's dead?' I could hear the sirens coming closer.

Charlie stood up and wiped her hands on the front of her jeans before approaching Freddie's lifeless form. She peered at him from a few feet away.

'I think he's had a heart attack.'

The sirens were really close now, heralding the arrival of the law. I scrambled to my feet and staggered towards my sister. Relief coursed through me. It was over. We were alive.

'I thought we were going to die.' I hugged Charlie as tightly as I could. I could smell the lovely familiar scent of her designer shampoo, reassuringly normal and comforting.

'I know, I did too. I'm so sorry, Abbey. What the hell were we thinking? Why did I ever let you and Kip get sucked into this?' Tears coursed down her face and dripped on to my old-lady blouse, soaking the collar where we were hugging.

'It wasn't your fault.' I tried to console her. It had been all three of us. We'd come up with this stupid plan together.

'I'm the eldest, it's up to me to look after you and Kip. I've made such a mess of everything. I've mucked up things between me and Philippe and you and Mike, Kip ran away and now I got us both shot at.' She gulped.

'It's okay. It's over now.' I wiped the tears from her cheeks with my fingers.

'It's not okay. We were nearly killed. You were so brave.'

'I wasn't brave. I thought he was going to shoot you.' I hadn't been brave at all. I hadn't even thought about the consequences of my actions when I'd launched myself at Freddie. All I'd seen was my sister in danger.

At the entrance of the churchyard, torches had appeared and male voices broke the eerie stillness.

'We're over here! There's been an accident, we need an ambulance.' Charlie broke free and hailed the police, who raced across the graveyard towards us. As they got nearer I saw that Mike was with them, leading the way. He was heartbreakingly familiar in his faded denims and white T-shirt, seemingly impervious to the chilly air.

'Who's hurt?' He tripped on a hidden stone and cursed as he hurried over to us. I could see him looking around as he drew closer. 'Where's Abbey?'

A tiny glow of warmth flickered inside me. He still cared enough to be concerned. He'd asked about me.

'She's here. We're both okay,' Charlie called. 'It's Freddie, he collapsed. We think he's dead.' She shivered.

Mike slowed to a walk and headed straight over to Freddie, falling on to one knee while he checked for a pulse. He scowled when he saw the gun lying where it had fallen in the long grass.

'What happened?' He dropped Freddie's lifeless hand and got to his feet. His colleagues came panting into the small clearing next to the rubbish heap to join him.

One of the policemen got straight on his radio

when he saw Freddie's body, while another examined the angel's wing that had been chipped and cracked by the stray bullet.

'He threatened us with the gun. Then he tried to shoot us but he had a heart attack.' Charlie still had her arm round my waist.

'What the hell did you think you were playing at?' he demanded. 'You could have been killed.'

'We're sorry. We wanted to try to catch him to show you we're not really bad people.' I choked on the lump in my throat.

Mike peered at me. 'Who's that?' He came a step closer. 'Abbey?' His voice sounded incredulous.

I pulled off my grey curly wig and took the grips out of my hair so it fell loose around my shoulders, then I rubbed at the thick stage make-up on my face.

'What on earth have you two been doing?' Mike shook his head in disbelief.

'We had this plan,' I tried to explain.

'I bet you did.' Mike didn't sound impressed.

'Charlie! Abbey!' Kip hurried towards us, accompanied by one of the Spanish bodyguards and Mike's colleague Diane. A veritable swarm of people appeared around us. Radios crackled and someone started to photograph Freddie's body. We moved away to meet Kip, desperate to stop him from seeing it.

'It's all right, we're okay. It's over.' We hugged amongst the gravestones.

The bodyguard pulled out his phone and began talking to someone.

'It's not finished yet. You lot have got some serious explaining to do,' Mike said.

We spent a long time at the police station; the questioning went on all night. By the time we had all been interviewed about the events of the evening and our connection to Freddie I was exhausted. Charlie had called the solicitor Philippe had sent over just a couple of days earlier and asked him to come to the police station to advise us.

I wondered how we would manage to pay for his services as he didn't look like the kind of professional who came cheap. Kip said we would get legal aid but I couldn't see it myself. Especially not enough to pay a man who wore Hugo Boss suits and expensive shoes, but now wasn't the time to worry about how we were going to afford him.

Eventually we were allowed to go, after we'd promised not to leave the area and to return to the police station in the week for further questioning. Charlie called us a taxi and we headed home. It was mid-morning and I wanted my bed. All the adrenalin that had kept me going for the past twelve hours had left me and I was exhausted.

Our bodyguards had disappeared after they'd seen we were safely in police custody. I'd heard one of them on his mobile in the cemetery. He'd been speaking Spanish so I'd assumed he had been reporting in to Philippe. His mama would no doubt be relieved that her son could sever all connections with us now that Freddie was dead and we were out of danger. I wondered how Philippe himself felt.

I stared at my reflection in the bathroom mirror before washing the remains of the stage make-up from my face. It was no wonder Mike had looked so stunned when he'd seen me in my little old lady get-up. With my hair hanging lankly round my shoulders and the thick pancake foundation all smeared and blotchy from my attempts to rub it off I looked like a crazy old bag-woman.

For a brief moment when he'd run towards us in the graveyard asking where I was, I'd really hoped that maybe, just maybe, there was a microscopic chance of us getting back together. He had seemed genuinely concerned; I couldn't have been mistaken about that, could I? I squirted liquid soap on to my hand and worked it up into a foamy lather. Who was I trying to kid? Looking at it logically there was no way we could be together.

I washed the remainder of the make-up from my skin and patted my face dry with a towel. With all the gunk gone I could see the dark circles under my eyes that had been caused by the lack of sleep. I was Abigail Gifford again. Ordinary looking, the kind of girl you'd pass by in a crowd. Ordinary height, ordinary hair, with an average figure, nothing to make a bloke like Mike look twice. I'd simply been fooling myself.

Kip knocked on the bathroom door. 'Hurry up, Abbey.'

I undid the lock and let him in. Claude skittered in behind him in his exercise ball, his ratty whiskers twitching as he rolled up next to the bath.

'I'm glad you didn't die.' The Adam's apple in Kip's throat bobbed as he swallowed. It was a classic Kip response.

'So am I.'

'I don't want to live on a farm any more. Not if it means you and Charlie are going to be murdered.'

'I think the farm idea is gone anyway, Kip, and Charlie and I have no intention of being murdered.'

'Does that mean you aren't going to do any more scams?' He looked relieved.

'I think we've retired from our life of crime.' With any luck we had, anyway. I think even Charlie had finally had enough after everything we'd been through. There had to be another way.

It was early evening when I finally woke and went downstairs. My throat felt dry and scratchy and, sure enough, a large purple bruise had appeared on my hip from my fall in the graveyard.

Charlie was already in the kitchen. 'Kip's still asleep.' She poured me a cup of tea.

'How are you feeling?' Unusually for my sister, she hadn't bothered to put on her make-up and her hair hung limp and unbrushed in a loose ponytail. Like me, she was still wearing her nightclothes.

'I've had days when I've felt better.' She forced a smile.

'Did the solicitor say what he thought would happen now?' She had dealt with most of the legal issues while we had been in custody. I had simply answered all the questions they'd asked and worried about Kip.

Charlie shrugged. 'It all depends. They were going to do a post-mortem on Freddie but the doctor who attended the scene said he was pretty certain it was a massive heart attack. The only evidence against us of any kind of crime is our confession to scamming Freddie. Since he's dead, he's not in a position to make a complaint and there's not likely to be any evidence of money missing from his account that could be traced to us.'

'What about any other charges?' It all seemed complicated to me.

'What charges? We haven't been charged with anything. We might have planned to scam Philippe and raid his safe but we didn't actually *do* anything. I didn't tell them anything about our plans, did you?'

I shook my head. 'They didn't ask anything specific about Philippe.'

'Then I guess that's okay. Did they ask you about anything else?' She took a sip from her drink.

'No. They asked about Freddie, that was all.'

She replaced her mug on the breakfast bar. 'I suppose we'll have to wait and see what happens, then.'

'Did they talk to Kip?' He could have told them anything depending on what questions had been put to him.

Charlie shook her head. 'I was there with the solicitor when they spoke to him. It was really only to confirm what I'd told them.'

I drank my tea and thought about what she'd said. I suppose the likelihood of our not being charged with any offence looked quite good from our point of view.

'Have you heard anything from Philippe?' I'd wondered if the bodyguards' report on the happenings of last night might have prompted him to get in touch.

She shook her head. A single tear ran down her cheek and plopped on to the breakfast bar. She grabbed a sheet of kitchen towel and blew her nose.

'It's over, Abbey. I really, really liked him, you know. I don't think I would have gone through with our plan.'

Her words confirmed what I'd suspected from the start. The way she'd acted around him and spoken about him had been a dead giveaway. I knew she'd allowed herself to fall in love. The way I'd fallen in love with Mike.

'Have you spoken to Aunty Beatrice?' That was something else that had been bothering me. If any of last night's activities made the news – and there was a good chance they would – then she needed to be prepared.

'I called her earlier. I didn't go into everything in detail, obviously.' She paused and pulled a face. 'But I told her Freddie was dead and that it had been quite dramatic.'

That was an understatement. 'How did she take it?'

Charlie sighed and tucked a loose strand of hair behind her ear. 'As well as you might expect. I got a lecture that lasted half an hour, and she threatened to make Kip live with her as I was clearly irresponsible and you were obviously going the same way. She was disappointed in both of us, and so on and so forth.' She waved her hand, indicating that it had been the usual dressing-down with knobs on.

The ring of the front doorbell startled us both.

'Finish your drink. I'll go, it's probably Sophie.' Charlie slipped her feet into her fuzzy pink slippers and padded off towards the hall.

A few seconds later, Philippe was standing in the

kitchen. I made my excuses and fled upstairs with the remainder of my tea, leaving my shell-shocked sister with her unexpected guest.

Kip emerged from his room in his pyjamas. 'Who was at the door?'

'Philippe.'

'The match must have finished, then. I didn't realise it was that time already.' He yawned and raked his hands through his curls, making them appear even crazier than usual.

I'd forgotten that Philippe was supposed to be playing today. He must have headed here as soon as the last whistle had been blown. Whatever he wanted to see Charlie about had to be pretty important for him to miss out on the post-match shindig and rush straight here.

'I thought I'd better leave them alone to talk.'

'I wanted a cup of tea.' Kip eyed my mug.

I handed him my drink.

'Thanks, Abbey.' He disappeared back into his room.

I wished I could be a fly on the wall so that I could hear what Philippe was saying to Charlie, but since I couldn't do that my only option was to lurk on the landing like a lemon until I judged it was safe to go back downstairs. Failing that, I could take a nice long bath. Naturally enough, the bath won.

The front door closed while I was in the middle of blow-drying my hair. I switched off the dryer and headed back to the kitchen with half my hair still dripping wet. Charlie met me in the doorway with a watery smile and a big hug.

'What happened? What did he say?'

She wiped her eyes with her hand. 'He came to make up. He said he'd been thinking about everything and he'd heard all about what happened last night from Father O'Mara.'

I must have looked bewildered. My sister grabbed my hands and pulled me on to the sofa in the lounge. 'He said he'd been worried when the bodyguards had called him after the explosion at the house.'

'I didn't think of that.'

'Then they called him from the cemetery when they arrived with Kip and the police. Father O'Mara had told him all the details about how we'd tackled a dangerous killer in the churchyard.'

'How did Father O'Mara know what had happened?'

'Philippe says the police called him as Freddie had died in church grounds.'

'And Philippe still loves you?' I was really happy for her. I couldn't help wishing Mike had called round to say the same sort of things to me.

Charlie nodded. 'Bella doesn't approve, though.' Charlie's face clouded. 'She told Philippe he would never be able to trust me.'

I blinked. 'That was a bit strong.'

Charlie grimaced. 'I couldn't argue, could I? Not after everything I'd confessed to him about how I'd set out to make him notice me and why.'

True, but I still thought it was a bit much. 'He must really love you to override Bella.'

'I know.' My sister blushed. 'I wish she'd give us her blessing, though. I don't want to be on bad terms with her. She's not the kind of woman you'd want as an enemy.'

I gave her a hug. 'She'll change her mind when she gets to know you better. I suppose that means we have to go to church tomorrow?'

'And on Monday. Father O'Mara is conducting Mum's memorial Mass that afternoon, remember? We all have to be there for that.' She squeezed my fingers.

'Okay.' I couldn't say I was looking forward to either event. It would be hard to sit through the services with everyone staring at us. I was quite sure that the story of our adventures amongst the graves would have circulated far and wide by now.

Philippe was waiting for us the next day at the church. He stood alone at the entrance, smiling and saying hello to the congregation as they entered. As soon as he saw Charlie his face lit up and he came over to kiss her cheek. We'd left Kip at home as there was no way he would cope with attending a service two days in a row and we felt it was more important that he came to the memorial Mass. Philippe, Charlie and I entered the church together with our heads held high.

Bella was already seated in her usual pew with Maria. As Philippe took his seat next to Charlie instead of with his mother, the little girl turned round and gave us a tiny wave. Bella continued to sit with her head firmly turned away from us, her eyes seemingly fixed on the altar. It didn't look as if she was going to mellow any time soon.

The theme of the service was forgiveness. I had long suspected Father O'Mara of having a wickedly dry sense of humour. I'm sure it was no coincidence that his kindly smile was often directed towards Bella as he spoke.

He announced Mum's memorial Mass at the end of the service, adding that he hoped members of the congregation would try to attend to support us through this difficult time. We had still received no word from the coroner's office about when Mum's body would be released for burial, so at least the Mass would give us some kind of closure.

Bella exited the church without acknowledging us at all. It didn't look as if the hints Father O'Mara had dropped during the service had made much impact. A few people murmured sympathetic comments to us as we left. Philippe walked with us as far as the lychgate. It looked different in daytime, beautiful and peaceful.

'I will talk again with Mama,' Philippe assured Charlie. 'She forgets that her own papa was not a pillar of the community.'

I remembered what Charlie had told me ages ago about the origins of the money and jewellery in Bella's safe. Perhaps Philippe had a point. If Bella's father had been no angel then she could hardly criticise Charlie for behaving in a similar way. Like Philippe's grandfather, Charlie had simply been trying her best to provide for her family.

Looking across the graves we could see the bright plastic tape marking the scene of the incident. I felt sick when I saw it, incongruous and stark against the grey stones. Charlie and I had come very close to ending up dead like our mother that night. A shudder ran through my body as I remembered Freddie lying sprawled on the wet grass. We were very lucky to be alive.

Philippe kissed Charlie goodbye and went off to take his mother and sister home.

'I'm so glad you two are back together.' I slipped my arm through Charlie's and we set off on the long walk back to our house. We hadn't yet had a chance to sort out a replacement for our poor exploded VW. Luckily, it was a dry day with the sun peeping out from behind the fluffy clouds scudding across the sky. The leaves on the large trees lining the edges of the pavement were starting to turn a rich golden yellow and the smell of autumn was in the air.

'Thanks. I wish it had worked out between you and Mike.' She glanced at me.

I wished it had worked out, too. I wondered if I would ever see Mike again. Pain still hit me, as sharply as a physical wound, whenever I thought about him. I felt exhausted emotionally by everything I'd gone through. For all I knew he could be back in London already.

We turned off the main road to walk along the side street where I'd stolen the dahlias. I felt a pang of guilt when I noticed the bare patch amongst the floral display. A car horn sounded behind us, making us both turn our heads to see who it was.

'Can I give you a lift?' Mike's car slowed to a crawl beside us. The roof was down and he steered the car lazily towards the kerb with one hand. My heart gave a leap of delight, even though I couldn't tell from his face whether this was to be business or pleasure. Charlie nudged me.

'I thought I'd warned you before about kerb-crawling.' What a stupid thing to say. It was like a rerun of the day he'd offered me a lift home from the park. I couldn't believe he was there.

'If you got in I wouldn't be kerb-crawling.' He put his hazard lights on so the cars behind would overtake him. The corner of his mouth quirked upwards and I knew he'd remembered too. My legs had gone a bit wobbly and my pulse raced.

'Get in the car!' Charlie hissed in my ear. She gave

me a little push in his direction before announcing: 'I'll walk home. Bye, Abbey.' She dropped my arm and quickened her pace to leave me behind.

'Well?' Mike's dark eyes locked into mine.

My stomach gave a funny little flip. I ran round the front of the car, opened the passenger door and jumped in. He pulled out and swung the car round in a three-point turn, screeching the tyres slightly as we headed away from my house.

'Where are we going?' I couldn't quite believe that he had come to meet me.

'Somewhere quieter where we can talk.'

I studied him covertly as he drove, trying to work out what he might have to say to me. I didn't dare hope that there might still be a chance for us. At least I should be grateful that he hadn't come to arrest me.

It wasn't long before he parked the car in a small car park surrounded by tall, leafy trees. We were the only car on the lot and the only sound was the twittering of the birds on the branches high above our heads.

'I wanted to tell you myself but you should hear this officially from your solicitor soon. The view of the officers in the case is that we haven't any evidence against you or your sister. There won't be any formal charges laid against either of you.'

Disappointment washed over me. This was official business after all.

'Thank you.'

'It seemed only right that I should be the person to let you know.'

'I didn't think you wanted to see me again.' I couldn't read how he might be feeling about me. Did he regret getting involved with me? Kissing me? I wished I had carried on walking home with Charlie. Sitting here in this intimate space with Mike was breaking my heart.

'I wasn't sure which Abbey I was likely to see. The Abbey I thought I was beginning to get to know – a sweet, honest girl with amazing eyes – or con woman Abbey, the human chameleon and accomplished actress.' He swivelled in his seat to face me.

Ouch. It was a fair comment, I supposed, although I couldn't help liking the part about having amazing eyes. A tiny glimmer of hope had pinged into life at that bit.

'Who are you, Abbey?'

I wasn't sure I could have answered that question a few weeks ago, but the things that had happened to me lately had done a lot to clear my mind.

'I'm Abigail Elizabeth Gifford. I was hit by lightning and I can't lie when you ask me a question, so only ask me questions when you're sure that you really want to know the answers.' I met his gaze with my own, daring him to ask me whatever he wanted.

I made a mental plea bargain with God that if Mike wanted to carry on seeing me I'd be willing to stay honest for ever and ever. I'd half expected him to smile at my answer but instead he stayed looking serious.

'There are a lot of questions I'd like to ask you.'

'Are you prepared for the consequences?' We both knew that I had no choice but to tell him the truth. I swallowed hard.

'I'm prepared.' His voice held that same slightly gruff, sexy rumble that had melted my heart when we'd first met. He might be prepared for the fallout from whatever questions he wanted to put to me but I wasn't certain I was.

'Then ask away.' I tried to keep my tone light but instead I sounded squeaky.

A flicker of emotion showed in his dark eyes. 'Are you the same girl I started falling in love with the moment I first saw her in a hotel bar?'

My mouth dried and my stupid heart fluttered. 'I'm that girl.'

'Have you and Charlie given up any planned criminal activities?'

'Yes.' I hardly dared to breathe.

He leaned slowly towards me and kissed me on the lips. A tingle of desire starting from my mouth spread through my body. 'No more scams?' His tone was firm but his eyes were twinkling.

'No more scams.'

He kissed me again, making my body fizz with pleasure. My heart swelled with happiness at being back in his arms.

'Would you like to go out for dinner tomorrow night?'

This time I answered him by kissing him back.

We arrived at the church for Mum's memorial Mass the following afternoon. Butterflies fluttered in my tummy when Father O'Mara met us at the door. This was almost the final step in closing the door to our past. Charlie had convinced Kip that he had to attend and Sophie's father had given her his permission to join us.

Mike had said he'd meet us at the church and Philippe had his coach's blessing to cut his training session short so he could support Charlie. True to their words both men were waiting, dressed in dark suits and sombre ties, next to Father O'Mara. As soon as Mike held my hand I started to feel better. Philippe slipped a supportive arm round Charlie as we steeled ourselves for the service.

We weren't sure that anyone else would be there, despite Father O'Mara's invitation. However, as we entered the dimly lit interior of the church we found half a dozen members of the congregation waiting to support us. More important – especially where Charlie was concerned – sitting in her usual pew was Bella.

I knew she wouldn't have come if she hadn't been prepared to accept Charlie, and glancing at my sister I could see the emotion in her eyes at the sight of her.

Philippe's talk and Father O'Mara's sermon must have had a positive effect after all.

Mike held my hand, Philippe held Charlie's hand and as I peeped along the pew I saw that Sophie had hold of Kip's hand, too. As Father O'Mara began the service and we prayed for Mum, it looked as if we were all finally going to get our normal life.

Pick up a *little black dress* – it's a girl thing.

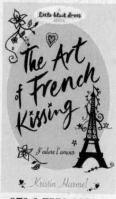

THE ART OF FRENCH KISSING
Kristin Harmel
PB £4.99

When Emma lands her dream job in Paris, she starts to master the art of French kissing: one date, one kiss and onto the next delectable Frenchman. But what happens if you meet someone you want to kiss more than once . . .

A très chic tale of Paris, paparazzi and the pursuit of the perfect kiss

978 0 7553 3828 3

THE CHALET GIRL
Kate Lace
PB £4.99

Being a chalet girl is definitely not all snowy pistes, sexy ski-instructors and a sensational après-ski nightlife, as Millie Braythorpe knows only too well. Then handsome troublemaker Luke comes to stay at her chalet and love rages, but can he be trusted or will her Alpine romance end in wipeout?

978 0 7553 3831 3

Pick up a *little black dress* – it's a girl thing.

978 0 7553 3959 4

TANGLED UP IN YOU
Rachel Gibson
PB £4.99

Sex, lies and tequila slammers

When Maddie Dupree arrives at Hennessy's bar looking for the truth about her past she doesn't want to be distracted by head-turning, heart-stopping owner Mick Hennessy. Especially as he doesn't know why she's really in town . . .

SPIRIT WILLING, FLESH WEAK
Julie Cohen
PB £4.99

Welcome to the world of Julie Cohen, one of the freshest, funniest voices in romantic fiction!

When fake psychic Rosie meets a gorgeous investigative journalist, she thinks she can trust him not to blow her cover – but is she right?

978 0 7553 3481 0

You can buy any of these other
Little Black Dress titles from your
bookshop or *direct from the publisher*.

FREE P&P AND UK DELIVERY
(Overseas and Ireland £3.50 per book)

TO ORDER SIMPLY CALL THIS NUMBER

01235 400 414

or visit our website: www.headline.co.uk

Prices and availability subject to change without notice.